SINFUL ATTRACTION

A TEMPERANCE FALLS ROMANCE

LONDON HALE

SINFUL *attraction*

LONDON HALE

LONDON HALE

*Dedicated to the companies that make huge
hot water heaters, because shower sex would be
uncomfortable without you.*

chapter one

WHO'D HAVE THOUGHT this was what I'd be doing on a Thursday night? That I'd be following a girl around like some kind of fucking creeper, using every one of my resources as a cop to keep tabs on her. To make sure she was safe.

But then again, it wasn't just any girl. It was Lola Perez. The woman who'd haunted my dreams for the past two years since she'd moved in to the apartment below mine in the four-plex we shared. A woman who was far too sweet for me. Too young. Too innocent. Too *good*.

In the time we'd spent together as friends since she'd moved in—a shared pizza here, some Netflix binge-watching there—I'd come to find she wasn't much younger than I was, but she had a fresh-faced innocence about her that reminded me so much of my sister. Combine that with how I'd found Lola last week, tugged into an alley off Main Street by a man she obviously didn't want to be with…the fear and blind panic on her face—

Jaw clenching, I shoved the thoughts away as I pushed through the front door of the church, a sense of calm washing over me as soon as my eyes landed on her. Just like always, she sat in the last pew. Never the middle or the front. Always the last pew on the right, head bowed, hands clasped in her lap, her long, dark hair falling forward to conceal her face from onlookers. I didn't need to see it, though. I'd studied her long enough to have her features memorized. Bright eyes—vibrant green irises with a starburst of fire around her pupil—pink, curved lips, and the barest hint of a dimple when she smiled. God, I loved making her smile.

The first time I'd found her sitting alone in the church had been complete happenstance. It'd been only a couple weeks ago as I'd been patrolling the area during Jane's Hour at Sin. I'd walked past the church just as someone had been leaving, the door opening as they'd stepped out. And there she'd been, looking sad…lonesome. Like a moth to a flame, I'd slipped inside and sat down next to her. Not to talk. Not to ask her what she was doing there or why she came. Simply to sit. To offer her companionship—the same thing I'd been doing every day since she'd moved in to the four-plex. Letting her know she wasn't alone.

Our relationship had evolved from something neighborly to something much deeper over the course of the two years since she'd stepped foot in my life. And I'd spent almost the entirety of that time attempting to avoid the attraction between us. Fighting it and pushing it away. But there was no getting around the fact that we'd been drawn to each other like magnets—always had been.

Now, though, I was tired of fighting the pull.

If last week had taught me anything, it was that life could change in the blink of an eye. If I hadn't been there in time…if I'd been even five minutes later—

"You don't have to come, you know," she said, her voice a whispered breath in the sanctuary.

I glanced over at her, cataloging her features—features that had starred in a hundred dreams. She'd tucked her hair behind her ear, and I wanted to reach out and see if her face felt as soft as it looked. Wanted to swipe my thumb over her full bottom lip. Wanted to taste it on my tongue.

Instead, I answered her the only way I ever did. I slipped my arm behind her across the back of the pew, careful to give her the space she so obviously craved. But just like always, I let only my thumb brush against her shoulder, the softest, barest touch. Reassuring her she wasn't alone in the most unobtrusive way I could. Even through the layers of her clothes and the long coat she still wore, she felt the contact—she always did. Her whole demeanor changed at that first brush of my thumb against her. She relaxed into the pew, her shoulders sagging as if she'd been carrying the weight of the world on them.

Sometimes we sat for five minutes, sometimes forty-five. It was random, no rhyme or reason to the timing that I could see, but I was there however long she needed.

Tonight, she stood after about ten minutes, tugging her coat tighter around her, concealing whatever she wore underneath. And then she walked toward the exit, never once glancing back to see if I'd follow her. She didn't need to. I was always there.

Since the first time I'd found her here, we'd fallen into a certain rhythm. I'd sit next to her for however long she needed, follow her out to the parking lot, and make sure she got home okay. Most of the time, we'd hang out at my place, order some Chinese or a pizza, and binge-watch a show on Netflix. We'd developed an easy camaraderie between us, even as I buried the part of me that wanted nothing more than to feel her under me. To know what her curves felt like under my hands. But since the night last week, everything had been thrown into chaos. I didn't just want to make sure she was safe, I *needed* to.

I walked close to her, using my body to shield her much smaller one from the biting January wind. "Why haven't you been answering your door when I've knocked?"

She didn't look back. Didn't pause as she hustled toward her car. "I've been studying."

Looking down at her, I raised an eyebrow. "You can't answer the door when you're studying? We haven't hung out at all this week."

She shrugged, not once glancing over at me.

"I study with headphones on. I probably didn't hear you."

Lola was good at avoidance—I'd found that out in the past several days…ever since I'd pulled that guy off her in the alley. She wasn't lying, that much I was certain of. But just the same, I wouldn't put it past her to intentionally study with her headphones on so she could use it as an excuse and wouldn't *have* to answer the door.

Her car was parked under the light in the church parking lot, the pile of junk a thorn in my side. I hated that she drove a piece of shit older than she was, knowing it was a breath away from dying on the side of the road and leaving her stranded.

"I'll follow you home. You want to order a pizza?"

The change was subtle—just a slight tightening of her shoulders—but I saw it all the same. "I can't. I have…plans."

She'd always been vague and evasive, giving just enough information to pacify me, but this was different. The undercurrent of nervousness was something new. Normally, I would've let it go. Prior to last week, I wouldn't have thought anything of it. I would've hated knowing she was out there without me, but I'd have dealt with it. Now, though? After peeling that fucker off her, after seeing the bruises on her wrist from where he'd grabbed her? I *couldn't* let it go.

"What kind of plans?"

She exhaled a deep sigh as she unlocked her door, her irritation visible. "That's not really your business, Connor."

I worked hard not to let my frustration show. Something was up, but I couldn't quite figure it out. It could've been in response to what had happened—I'd watched my sister pull away in the same manner after her attack. But a niggling voice told me something else was going on here. If my instincts were correct—which they usually were—I was missing an important piece, and I was almost certain it had to do with her job.

Since she'd moved here, she'd told anyone who asked that she worked from home doing sales for a marketing firm on the mainland. But that didn't explain where she went at night. Didn't explain the schedule she kept or her evasiveness whenever her job came up.

Reaching out, I wrapped my fingers around her wrist, tugging her to a stop before she could get into her car. "I just want to make sure you're safe, Lo."

She smiled, but it didn't reach her eyes. Didn't draw out her dimple. "I'll be fine. If I get done early, I'll come up and say hi. We can watch a movie or something. Okay?"

No, it wasn't okay. Even a little. But I'd been there before and knew there was no getting around it. No getting information out of her. She was stubborn almost to a fault—something we had in common— and wasn't going to give in, no matter how much I sweet-talked her.

I held open the car door for her, waiting for her to slide into the seat and buckle her seat belt. "I'm counting on it."

She didn't look at me, didn't glance up with a

smile like she normally would have. She just waited for me to step out of the way so she could shut the door. Then she started her car and drove off.

And I did the only thing I could. I followed her.

Always careful to stay just at the speed limit, she made her way toward the north end of the island. All that was up this way in Temperance Falls was a small horse farm, an apple orchard, and the farmer's market when it was in season. But it turned out she wasn't staying in Temperance Falls. The feeling of unease settling in my gut only grew when she turned toward the bridge, then went straight over it toward the mainland. Being careful to keep distance between us, I followed her into a nice neighborhood, large houses and well-kept lawns lining the streets.

She parked at the curb in front of a two-story brick colonial, forcing me to stop a couple houses down. Her lights went off, and there she sat. Minutes ticked by, and still no movement came from her car.

"What are you doing, Lo?" I whispered to myself as I surveyed the street, looking for anything out of the ordinary. Always keeping a watch for any threats.

And then her door opened and she stepped out, glancing around before she tucked her chin close to her chest and walked up to the front door of a house a few down from where she'd parked. My entire body grew taut, not knowing what awaited her when that door opened. Hating not being able to see the face of whoever answered. Hating even more as she slipped through the door, and then she was out of my sight.

I sat there for long minutes, eyes glued to the

front door, waiting. For what, I wasn't sure. A sign she was okay. A sign she wasn't.

The longest thirteen minutes of my life passed before that door flew open and out ran Lola. The scene was so reminiscent of years ago—of my sister running from a house so similar to this one, of me not being there in time to stop her horror—it took me by surprise. I sat frozen, unsure what to do, until someone stormed out of the house after Lola. I was out of my car before I could blink, sprinting toward her.

chapter two

LOLA

IF THERE WAS one thing I hated about my life, it was having to lie to Connor Nash. Okay, there was plenty more to hate. I was living half a continent away from my family, taking a double course load at Temperance Falls College to get my degree quickly, and working a job that sucked the soul right out of me most days. Technically, I lied to everyone I ran into. Or at least, stretched the truth.

What do you do? Sales.

Where do you work? From home most days, unless I need to visit a client.

What are you doing Saturday night? Working.

Well, that one was often the truth, and it created a huge barrier between me and any sort of dating possibility. The hazards of being a sex worker.

Of course, not dating simply meant more time

for crushing on my neighbor. Connor was the epitome of a woman's fantasy partner come to life: tall, handsome, sweet, caring, a little overprotective at times but in a good way. He was my best friend on the island…my only friend. He was also the only man I'd ever pictured myself having a relationship with, though there was no way that could happen. Connor was a cop, and I…well, I sold sexual fantasies for a living.

Not a good combo.

I headed for the bridge, not wanting to deal with ferry timetables and schedules tonight. Pulling myself from my usual Connor-and-me-happily-ever-after dream and back into my reality. I had a date with a John. Well, not a date, really. More an appointment.

Ever since I'd moved on from actual sex acts to working only the kink and fantasy squad, I couldn't think of my working hours as dates. I mean, no one would date the guy who only wanted you to wear yoga pants and wiggle your butt on his face, right? No one would date the man who liked a woman to wear skimpy lingerie and no shoes so he could perform a dental exam on her toes. The men were usually nice and the pay was phenomenal, but the weird factor was pretty high. Not high enough to go back to earning a living spreading my legs and giving blow jobs, mind you, but high. And I had a feeling it was changing my opinions of men in general.

All men except Connor. He was a bright spot no matter how dark my days and nights became. Someone who'd sort of adopted me when I'd moved in to the building after my family had moved back to Ecuador. He'd taken care of me when no one else bothered, and I'd lied to him…again. Like always. He was a cop—he couldn't know what I did for a living. If he hated me for it, if he turned me in, my life was over. If he didn't, and it was discovered that he'd looked the other way, his career would be. There was no happy medium for us except for me to keep lying.

"Four months to go," I whispered as I brought the Saint Christopher medallion hanging from my rearview mirror to my lips. It was a habit, one I'd developed a long time ago whenever I crossed over water. I hated bridges, hated the ferry, too. I hated that I had to leave the safety and security of Temperance Falls to go to the mainland for work.

Rumor, the woman who ran the escort agency, had tried to get me to work for clients on the island since I'd joined her staff, but I'd always refused… until I hadn't. There'd been one time, one meeting. Less than a week ago, I'd met a client on the island for an introductory get-to-know-you session, and everything had gone wrong. I'd been nervous, too worried about exposing myself to pay attention to him. The John had gotten handsy in public, a huge no-no for me. When I'd tried to end the meeting, he'd acted too possessive. Too…aggressive.

He'd had me pinned to the wall in an alley before I could even yell for help.

Connor showing up to save the day the way he always seemed to do had been both a blessing and a curse. A blessing because I'd been unable to protect myself from the wandering hands and the heavy weight of the man against me. A curse because I'd had to lie to Connor again. A hard lie that time, not an exaggeration. I'd told him I was on a date even though it broke my heart to say those words. But if he ever found out what I did to make money—if he knew the truth about me—our friendship would be over. Something I could not allow to happen.

Four months left. That was all I had of school, and then I could look for a real job. One that would pay me enough to afford my bills. One that didn't require me to take my clothes off or watch men jack off while I read the *Wall Street Journal* to them. One that didn't require me to rely on how young I looked to entice old men to live out some creepy teenage-reversion fantasy. Like I'd be doing tonight.

I drove past the John's house and parked at the end of the block. My heart raced, and my stomach churned as I prepared myself for what I had to do. For what I hated to do. This was my first client meeting since the potential John had attacked me on the island. The first time I'd been able to agree to handle a job. I'd turned away every request from new clients and occassionals, but I couldn't turn down this one. He was a regular—a weekly. I had to show up.

"You can do this," I told myself before pulling down the rearview mirror to apply the sickly sweet lip gloss he liked me to wear. I tucked my keys in the visor—I never liked to have them on me when I was in a client's house in case things went bad for me— and whispered, "You've got this."

Ten deep breaths, a fluff of my hair, and I was heading for his house. Thank God it was cold enough for me to wear my long winter coat. If Connor had seen the outfit I had on underneath—nope. I had to stop thinking about Connor. If I didn't, I wouldn't be able to go through with things. I wouldn't be able to put on the Lolita personality I used with these men. If I thought about Connor, I'd run back to the island and throw myself into his arms.

Best not to think about anything other than the cash.

The John, who I had always been told to call Davie, swung open the door before I could even ring the bell.

"There you are. I've been waiting for you. I'm so glad you could come for our playdate." His smile was as wide as ever, the costume he always wore childlike as usual. Dave had been a client for almost the entire two years I'd been working as an escort, and his particular fantasy was one of the easiest for me. He was the child, and I was the babysitter. We'd play in his toy room and eat kid-type snacks until it was time for his "nap," which was when he'd stroke himself while I danced around the room with headphones on. Weird, but not dangerous. Yet, that night, something felt off.

I hated feeling off.

"Hey, Davie," I said, my voice weaker than it should have been, my heart practically pounding in my throat. "I hope you're ready to play lots of board games tonight."

"Yes! I love board games." He moved back to let me inside and closed the door behind me.

The snick of the handle falling into place started me down the road to panic. Every instinct I had for self-preservation exploded at the sound. There was nothing out of the ordinary in his living room, nothing that should have concerned me, but that didn't stop the fear from pulling at me.

Still, I had a job to do. Four more months of them. I needed the money, and he needed me to be Lolita. Time to get to work.

"My parents will be back at ten," Dave said, tugging his too-tight shirt down over his expanding belly. "We've got hours to play, Lolita."

I cringed, the name making my skin crawl. "Perfect. Why don't you pick a game while I hang up my coat?"

The conversation continued as it always did, the scene playing out to his exact specifications. With every line, every word I had to speak in a singsong voice, my dread grew. But it was when Davie told me to follow him to the playroom—the bedroom he'd filled with child-sized furniture and shelves upon shelves of toys—that I broke.

It was a simple thing, really. A bag I noticed sitting on the kitchen table as we headed for the hallway. One with a logo I recognized from a shop on the island. From Connor's favorite bakery. In a split second, I went from Lolita the escort to Lola the girl in love with a man she couldn't ever have. How would Connor feel if he knew where I was, especially after he'd jumped in to save me last week? What would he think if he had any idea what I did when I told him I was working? Those soft touches and friendly evenings spent hanging out would disappear, that security blanket of his attention would implode. I would be alone…again. Always.

Fuck, what was I doing?

"Lolita?"

I jumped back, unable to stop thinking about Connor. Finding it impossible to move farther down the hall. "I'm sorry, but I need to go."

His confusion only made me feel worse. "But you're my babysitter."

I backed into the living room, my chest tight. The room seemed to spin, the air disappearing from my lungs as he stalked after me. "I'll have Rumor issue you a refund and a discount on a new appointment. I…can't."

"Excuse me?" Dave's smile fell, an angry scowl appearing on his round face. "We have an arrangement for tonight. I have everything prepared for us."

I hit the door without looking back. I couldn't be in that house a second longer. What was wrong with me? This was my job…the only way I had to make money to keep me on the island. If I couldn't do my job, what would I do? How would I survive?

How could I stay close to Connor if I couldn't pay my rent?

But in that moment, none of that mattered. I rushed down the sidewalk, heading for my car. The wind whipped past me, the cold biting into my legs.

Tight cotton shorts were not meant for this weather. The thin cropped shirt I wore didn't help either. My outfit bared far too much of my skin—I must have left my coat in the house. I couldn't care enough to go back. So long as I could get into my car, so long as I could escape…

"You fucking whore!" Dave's voice boomed through the night. "I've paid you good money for years, Lolita. You owe me."

I kept moving, refusing to look back. Practically running for my car. Almost there. Almost safe. If I could just get past the couple houses, if I could only hurry past these last few cars. If I could just—

I jumped as someone grabbed my arm, as a man pulled me off the sidewalk and toward an idling car at the curb. As Connor appeared out of nowhere.

Connor? "What—"

"Are you okay? Did he touch you? Did he hurt you?" His frantic voice broke through the panic in my head, though I still couldn't believe he was there. "Lo, *please*, tell me you're okay." His hands roamed over me, seemed on a mission to find…something. Maybe an injury, maybe a mark. But it was when he brought one hand to my face and gently wiped away the tears I'd apparently shed that I found my voice.

"It's okay. He didn't…" I shivered as the wind picked up again, my thoughts scattered, my mind unable to reconcile that Connor was there. Standing two houses down from where my John lived. I curled in on myself, trying to cover my bare stomach, wishing I'd grabbed my coat if only so he wouldn't see…this.

"C'mon." Ever the gentleman, Connor shrugged out of his heavy coat and wrapped it around my shoulders before moving me toward his car. He gave me no options; he didn't even let me speak. He simply opened the passenger door of his Charger and directed me inside. I was too upset to refuse, too cold to pull away. Too terrified of what he'd heard to do anything more than follow his directions.

Within seconds, he had my door closed and was sliding into his own seat. I couldn't even look at him, too afraid of the anger I'd see there. The disgust. Still, I had to know…

"Why are you here?" I asked, keeping my eyes on the passing houses as he drove out of the neighborhood.

"I'm here because you're here."

I hazarded a glance in his direction. His jaw was clenched, his fury obvious even in the darkness of the car. This would be it—I was going to lose him.

Unable to think about my life without him in it, I focused on the logistics of what had just happened. Had I quit my job? Yes, I think I had. I'd also just left my car behind. My coat, too. Shit.

I looked back at the floor and whispered, "What about my car?"

Connor pulled to a hard stop, the car rocking slightly as his hands gripped the steering wheel. "I'm not taking you back there. I *can't*. Please don't ask me to."

I shook my head because, really, I didn't want to go back either.

Connor took a deep breath, his voice a little calmer as he said, "I'll get my friend Nate to come over with me tomorrow, and we'll pick it up."

Okay. Connor would make everything okay. He was still my friend…so far. I looked up into his blue eyes. Barely able to breathe. Barely able to stop trembling. If I didn't have Connor in my life…

"Home or food?" he asked, his voice tight. His jaw ticking in that way it did when he was frustrated.

I licked my lips, the sick rising in my throat at the sticky sweetness there from the gloss. The gloss, the shorts and crop top…Lolita. I'd never wanted Connor to see me like this. But he had, and I needed to deal with the fallout. But not in his car, and definitely not off the island. "Take me home, please."

chapter three

CONNOR

THE SIGHT OF Lola fleeing that house, the terror on her face so reminiscent of the scene I'd come upon in the alley last week, wouldn't leave me alone. It replayed over and over in my mind as I sped us across the bridge toward Temperance Falls. Toward home. Lola had been terrified, without a doubt. And whatever had happened in that house…whatever had caused that fear…I hadn't been able to stop. I hadn't been able to protect her.

She spent the ride staring silently out the passenger window, never glancing my way. But at least she was no longer crying, so I took that as a good sign. At this point, I'd take any bit of good I could get.

When I pulled up along the curb in front of the four-plex, I went to her side and helped her out of the car. With an arm around her shoulders, I tucked her into my side and led her through the front door of the building. As if on autopilot, she headed toward her door, but that wasn't happening. No fucking way. After what happened tonight, I hated the idea of her being alone. But that wasn't exactly right, either. It wasn't just that I hated the idea of her being by herself. More, I hated the idea of her being where I wasn't. Not to mention the fact that she lived on the ground floor, shitty locks anyone could break her only protection. She was staying with me. Where I could keep her safe.

"You can stay at my place. At least until I can get your locks replaced, all right?"

With a distracted nod, she allowed me to lead her to my apartment. Walked in as if it were any other evening and we just had plans to watch some TV. But it wasn't any other evening. There was nothing normal about this. She didn't drop her coat and go over to the couch, making herself at home with her leg tucked under her like she usually would have. Instead, she stood only a couple steps in from my front door, her arms wrapped around herself, hiding in my too-big coat. Hiding the outfit she had on—short shorts and a crop top, reminiscent of some seventies style gym uniform. I had no idea why the fuck she was wearing something like that, but my cop senses had definitely been sparked. It was a piece to the Lola puzzle—I was sure of it. I just had to figure out how they all fit together.

I wanted nothing more than to walk over and wrap her in my arms, hold her to my chest to remind myself she was okay. So I could *feel* it. Feel her heartbeat against my chest, feel her breath on my skin. But she kept pulling the coat farther around her, tugging at the bottom as if she could make it longer. There wasn't a doubt in my mind she was uncomfortable. I just didn't know why. I didn't know if it was what had happened tonight—what she'd fled from. If it was me taking her home like some kind of jealous boyfriend. If it was the fact that she had on minuscule clothing under my coat. Regardless, I needed to make it better. Needed to make her feel settled. Safe.

"Are you hungry?"

No words. Just a simple shake of her head, her eyes still avoiding mine.

I had no idea what to do to make her feel comfortable. This was new territory for us. From the beginning, the very first day she'd moved in, we'd always been at ease around each other. It was almost eerie how effortlessly we'd fallen into a close friendship. Now there was a giant elephant in the room, and I didn't know how to address it.

"Do you wanna sit? Watch some TV?" As long as she was with me, I didn't care what we did.

She looked over her shoulder toward the door. "I need to go downstairs. I can't—" She shifted on her feet, tugging my coat closer around her. "I don't want to keep wearing this costume." Her voice caught on the last word, disgust dripping from her tone. If she had said nearly any other word, I wouldn't have thought anything of it. But it was that specific use that waved a red flag. Made my stomach sink with dread. Slotted more of those puzzle pieces into place.

The hours she kept, her secrecy, her aloofness the entire time we'd been friends, keeping me at arm's length even though I was sure I'd seen glimpses of longing on her face when she looked at me. The asshole running out after her tonight, calling her a whore… I'd been a cop long enough to see the commonality in the clues, to notice they were all pointing in the same direction. A direction I couldn't stand to think about. Not because I looked down on her for doing whatever she needed to to survive, but because I hated the idea of her doing anything that would compromise her safety.

"I've got something you can wear." My voice was rough, harsh thoughts making my words come out sharper than I'd intended. The last thing she needed tonight was to be bossed around. Getting my tone under control, I asked, "Is that okay?"

Those perfectly straight teeth sank into her bottom lip, brushed with some kind of sparkly pink gloss. It was so unlike her, I wanted to wipe it off myself. Wanted *my* Lo back. "Sure. Yeah."

With a nod, I led her into my bedroom, darting a glance around to make sure it was presentable. While she'd spent countless nights hanging out in my apartment, she'd never breached this boundary, never stepped foot into my bedroom. It'd been an unspoken agreement between us.

I hadn't bothered making my bed that morning, so the covers were rumpled, the pillows haphazard. I cringed, thinking I should at least get her clean sheets so she'd feel comfortable. But first, something for her to change into…

I grabbed her a sweatshirt from my drawer because she kept wrapping my coat tighter around her. I wasn't sure if it was because she was cold, or if it had more to do with the fact that she'd called what she wore under it a costume. It didn't matter. "I'll let you get changed."

She nodded. "Connor, I—"

I froze halfway through the doorway, my back to her as I waited for her to continue. When she didn't, I glanced back at her over my shoulder. "Yeah?"

She stared at me for a moment, then dropped her eyes and shook her head. "Nothing."

I wanted to let her know she could tell me anything. *Anything.* Even if it was the one thing I was pretty sure I'd already figured out. I wanted to tell her she could unload on me, cry, scream, rage, beat her fists against my chest—whatever she needed if it helped. Anything if it made her smile again. Instead, I nodded and walked out of the room, closing the door gently behind me.

Long minutes ticked by before the door opened and out she came, fingering the hem of my sweatshirt. She was petite—almost a foot shorter than I was—but her bare legs looked a mile long as they peeked out under the oversize sweatshirt. I wanted to feel those legs wrapped around my hips. Wanted them pressed against my ears as she came all over my tongue.

"Where should I sleep?"

Feeling like an asshole for even thinking about that after the night she'd had, I shook the fantasies from my head. "You can stay in my room tonight, and I'll sleep out here. Let me just change the sheets for you."

"Don't. There's no need to go to so much trouble."

I nodded, hating how much I loved the idea of her scent mixing with mine in my bed. "Tomorrow, I'll go to the hardware store and get replacement locks for your windows, okay?"

"You don't have to do that. Honestly."

I really did, though. I *had* to. In the two years she'd been in my life, somewhere along the way, I'd started to think of her as mine. "Yes, I do."

"Thank you." Her voice came out as a soft whisper, and then she turned away, the bedroom door snicking shut behind her.

I thought about her settling into my bed, into sheets that still smelled like me. Thought of her dark hair spilling over my pillow. Thought of what it'd be like to lay with her, curl myself around her, and… *comfort* her. There was no doubt I wanted to fuck her. Wanted to know what she felt like from the inside. Wanted to know if she liked having her clit sucked, if she liked having her tits played with. Wanted to know the noises she made when she came. But more than that, I wanted to make sure she knew she was safe with me.

Needing to get my mind off it, I did a quick pick-up of the living room. Changed out of my jeans and into a pair of sweat pants. Cleaned the bathroom counter. When none of that did anything to work off this excess energy, I headed into the kitchen and unloaded the dishwasher, trying to be quiet so as not to disturb her.

A couple minutes later, the bedroom door creaked open, and Lola poked her head out.

I froze in the middle of putting away the silverware. "Am I being too loud?"

She rested her cheek on the side of the door, her fingers curled around the edge, barely visible in the sleeves of my sweatshirt. "No, I…I can't sleep."

I shut the drawer and walked toward her. "How can I—what do you need?"

Darting her eyes to the side, she brought one foot to rest on the opposite ankle, drawing my attention to those legs I'd had so many fantasies about. "It's just… I'm not…" She blew out a breath. "It's so dark and quiet in there."

She was scared. Of course she was. After what happened tonight, I didn't blame her. "Would it help if I sat in there with you? Just until you fall asleep?"

Her eyes connected with mine, hitting me straight in the gut. So full of yearning. "Would you mind?"

I didn't answer, just walked toward her and guided her back into the bedroom. Wordlessly, she climbed into the bed, and I tried not to stare as I got a front row seat to the thoughts I'd had moments before. She curled on her side, pulling the comforter over her. Even though she'd covered more of herself from me, it only made my cock harden further. Knowing she was drawing comfort from my bed. Knowing exactly what was hiding under those blankets. I closed my eyes, attempting to get my thoughts under control, then went to the chair in the corner. I pulled it closer to the bed, ready to settle in for however long she needed. I'd sit there all fucking night if I had to.

"Can you—" She paused, her fingers playing with the edge of the blanket as she avoided my eyes. Then she lifted hers to meet mine. "Will you lie with me? Just for a little while?"

It wasn't a good idea. I knew it wasn't. My hard-as-fuck cock sure as hell knew it wasn't. But when she looked at me with those beseeching eyes, how could I say no?

I settled on my back next to her, wanting to offer her comfort with my presence but not wanting to overstep any boundaries. At first, I thought it was my imagination, how she kept inching closer. But soon, she was near enough that I could touch her if I reached out. So I did the only thing I could. I lifted my arm and placed it on her back, guiding her to tuck herself right into my side. She did so without hesitation, her legs tangled with mine, her head resting on my chest, hand settled on my stomach. And then, finally, she relaxed. Her body went boneless.

It was only when her breaths grew even, when I was sure she was asleep, that I allowed myself to tug her closer, loving the feeling of her in my arms. I pressed a kiss to the top of her head and fell asleep with my nose pressed to her hair, breathing in the scent of my Lo.

chapter four

LOLA

I WOKE UP in darkness, not quite conscious enough to think of anything other than how hot I was. Not a bad hot, like the summers back in Ecuador where the sun beat down on your head and the humidity tried to smother you. No, it was a comfortable warmth. A soft heat, one brought about by physical contact with someone else. By snuggling. A thought that brought me from half awake to fully awake in the blink of an eye.

Connor was wrapped completely around me. Or I was wrapped completely around him.

His arms—those muscled, freckled arms I'd noticed a million times since I'd moved in to the building—clutched me to his chest. So tight around me. So strong. He had his face buried in my neck and one calf lying across mine as if he wanted to touch every part he possibly could. All the parts I wanted him to touch.

But this was Connor…my neighbor and best friend. My only friend, really. As much as I wanted to stay there, to take advantage of every second of my own personal fantasy coming true, I knew he didn't mean to hold me like that. Connor was sweet and kind, a true caretaker. An overprotective bear of one, but a caretaker nonetheless. I couldn't take advantage of that trait.

I rolled back, slowly trying to extricate myself from his hold. Knowing I'd miss the heat of him as soon as there was space between us again. But Connor had other plans. He gripped me tighter, tugging me almost underneath him. We became connected from shoulders to toes, skin on skin where the shirt I slept in had pulled up. The trail of hair leading from his navel down into his sweat pants scratched against my stomach, and the weight of his thigh resting on top of mine pinned me in place. A fact I wasn't unhappy about.

There was nothing I could do, no way for me to escape him, so I lay in the dark and stared at the man I knew so well. He was handsome in his sleep. He was handsome all the time, but with his eyes closed and his jaw relaxed—with that sleepy-little-boy thing going on—he was irresistible. And I was so tired of resisting.

Giving in to my desire, hidden away as we were in the manufactured safety of his bedroom, I took a chance and reached for him. I ran a single finger down his cheek, smiling at the stubble that always darkened his jawline. He called it a five-o'clock shadow—I called it a five-day beard. I'd touched it before, teased him about his constant lack of shaving, but this was different. This was…sensual.

I touched, unable not to. Fearful I'd destroy everything, worried I was risking my heart and his career on the off chance of getting more. Wishing for things I could never have no matter how badly I wanted them. No matter how long I'd craved them.

Connor grunted in his sleep, his eyes fluttering as he pushed me onto my back and moved with me. Covering me. Laying his weight on me.

His weight, and his very hard, very large cock.

I froze, not sure what to do. I knew what I wanted to do, but he…he'd never looked at me as if he wanted me. Not really. Connor had never acted as if I were anything more than a friend. And after last night, after likely hearing that John call me a whore, I couldn't imagine he wanted me. His body betrayed those assumptions, though. And mine…well, it called to him. I was hot and wet for him already, and not just because of the temperature of his room.

"Lo," he mumbled, tugging me closer and brushing his nose along my cheek.

I closed my eyes and gripped his arm, something like desire brewing inside of me. Something unfamiliar in my life. It had been so long since I'd done anything physical for the sake of my own pleasure. Too long. I wasn't even sure if I remembered how to have a normal, sexual relationship with a man. I especially didn't know how to have one with a man like Connor. But I wanted one. Immediately. Desperately.

Digging deep to pull together every ounce of courage I had, I pushed against Connor's chest. He rolled, bringing me with him, his eyes popping open and meeting mine as he ended up flat on his back.

"Lola?"

I swung a leg over his hips, making sure to rub my thigh against where he was already so hard and hot. "Connor."

He groaned and tugged me until I was straddling him. Riding him. Only two thin layers of fabric between us.

"Lo…" Oh God, he groaned like he wanted. Like a man who needed. "What's this?" he asked as I rocked slightly, keeping my hips against his. Keeping that hard ridge trapped between us. I wanted to answer him honestly, to tell him I was offering myself to him. That I wanted him. That I'd always wanted him. But the words wouldn't come, my bravery petering out as my eyes adjusted to the low light in the room.

"What do you want it to be?" It was a dishonest sort of question, one that hid my own desire behind the possibility of his. He had to feel me against him. Had to know I was soaked for him.

"Oh Jesus. Don't ask me that, beautiful. Not when you're grinding your pussy on me. Please. I can't—" He shook his head, pulling me closer. Gripping my hips so tight I was sure he'd leave marks. Hell, I hoped he did.

Bravery and lust building into an inferno, I

dropped down and pressed my lips to his. Stole a kiss from the man I'd come to see as my true heart. It was soft and sweet…easy. No tongue, no open mouths or groping hands. A simple kiss. One that had been two years in the making. One that took everything I had to resist deepening.

"Please," I whispered, pulling away for just a second. He wouldn't let me, though. Wouldn't let me put an inch of space between us. He tugged me back down and pressed his lips to mine once more. This time, the kiss turned hot and lustful. Turned deep and languorous. Turned into the stuff of my fantasies.

Connor kissed me like I'd never been kissed before, his tongue sweeping into my mouth with purpose. Every inch of him seemed to tense beneath me as he grabbed and pulled and devoured. I held on to his shoulders, needing balance, rolling my hips against where he was so hard. I was too far gone, too deep into my need to think about the consequences of what we were doing. I wanted him, and from the way he groaned into my mouth as I ran my pussy along his cock, he wanted me as well.

"Fuck," Connor said as I pulled away from our kiss to catch my breath. He kept up his touching, though. Running his hands down to grasp my hips. Tugging my shirt—his shirt—up until we were flesh on flesh again. The feel of his skin against me, of his touch, had me rocking on top of him. Had me craving that release I had relinquished in my life. I hadn't come in years, hadn't even attempted to because of all the things I'd seen and done for my work. Hadn't wanted to. Connor made me want.

"I need—" I gasped, fighting off the orgasm I could feel building within me. "Connor, please."

"Take it, Lo." Connor lifted his hips, thrusting against me as he pulled me down and made me gasp. "Take what you need."

I couldn't resist another second. I pushed up, rolling my hips as I balanced with my hands against his chest. He pulled and pushed me, moving me over him, thrusting up every few passes to grunt and groan and make me feel so fucking good. Too good.

For the first time in two years, for one of the very few times in my life, I came. The orgasm roared through me, my muscles clenching in response. A deep, needy groan escaped my throat, one that seemed to push Connor closer to his own release as he bucked in response. And still, he held back. His face was pinched, his hands tight on me. I could almost feel his hesitancy, his slowing down. His withdrawal from me.

"Oh, Connor," I said, my brain a little foggy. My lips far too open and my secrets too accessible. "I've wanted this for so long."

Connor froze, his body stiffening. His eyes going wide. I stared down at him, breathing hard. My hands still pressed against his chest.

"Connor?"

Without a response, he growled and flipped me over, rutting against me in too fast, almost out of control thrusts. Filthy words fell from his lips, things like, "You soaked right through your panties, didn't you, beautiful? Can't believe you let me feel you come." I held on as best I could, my legs around his hips, my hands clutching at his shoulders as he bit and sucked and licked my neck. And then he groaned and pressed tight, his body rocking slightly. Jerking. Obviously coming.

Fuck, I'd made Connor come.

And I couldn't wait to do it again.

chapter five

CONNOR

I WOKE IN degrees of awareness. Warmth. The sun through the blinds? But there was softness, too. A body? Definitely a body. A hand resting gently on my stomach. Then a familiar scent that always reminded me of summer on the island washed over me. Lola.

Last night hit me with the force of a two-ton truck, snippets flashing through my mind like a flip-book. From the moment I'd found her sitting alone in the church to waking up in the middle of the night, Lola astride my hips, her pussy hot and so soft against where I'd been hard for her. Watching her take her pleasure from me. Hearing her whispered words telling me how long she'd wanted me.

I wanted to relish that thought, wanted to bask in it for a while, but I couldn't. Because mere hours before, she'd been running from a man. Crying.

Sobbing, really. And then I'd brought her home, gotten her safe, and…taken from her. I tried to remember if I'd done or said something to coerce her. If I'd taken advantage of her like some kind of insensitive asshole. The thought settled in my gut like lead, churning my stomach. I'd hate myself if she regretted anything that had happened between us.

She stirred in my arms, her body pressing closer as she tilted her head back, blinked open her eyes, and…smiled?

"Morning," she said, her voice still thick with sleep.

"Morning, beautiful." I reached up, brushed the hair from her face. Finally allowed myself to do what I'd thought about a hundred times and trailed my finger across her brow, down the curve of her cheek. Her skin was exactly as soft as it looked. And she was still smiling. At *me*.

The thought of her smile dimming—or worse, going out entirely—if there had been a different outcome last night… Jesus, I couldn't even think about the possibilities. I didn't know what I'd do if anything happened to her.

In the past two years, she'd come to mean so much more to me than just my neighbor, a woman new to town. What had started as a friendship loaded with attraction had transformed into something else, something more. And then last night had happened…

I've wanted you for so long.

Her whispered words as she'd been astride my hips, boneless from her orgasm, settled deep in my chest. Had that been a moment of sleep-induced confusion? Had she even meant to say it? Had she known it was me she'd said the words to?

Whatever her answers were, I had to know.

I brushed my thumb back and forth along her bottom lip. "Do you remember what you said last night?"

She paused long enough that I started to think maybe I'd made up the entire thing. But then she placed her palm flat on my chest, right over my heart, and whispered, "Yes."

"Did you mean it?"

With her fingers tracing a light circle on my chest, she stared up at me. Trying to get a read on me? On what I wanted to hear? I had no idea. Feeling the overwhelming urge to reassure her, I covered her hand with mine, using the other hand at the small of her back to press her closer.

After what felt like a lifetime, she said, "Yes." She licked her lips, her gaze dropping to my mouth for a moment. "I've always been attracted to you, Connor. It was never an option, though."

Hearing that she'd always been attracted to me went straight to my cock. As much as I wanted to give in to it, as much as I wanted to roll her under me and make her scream my name, we had more pressing issues. Things we needed to discuss—and not while in bed. So before she could feel exactly how much I wanted a repeat of what happened last night, I rolled out of bed, adjusting myself to make my erection less obvious.

She propped herself up on her elbow as she stared at me. "Where are you going?"

I wanted to crawl back under the covers with her, run my hands over her and feel her body tucked up against mine. Bury my face in her neck and inhale.

Later. First, breakfast.

"You didn't eat last night. I'm getting you food."

She raised her eyebrows, her lips curving. "With all the meals we've had together, you've never made me breakfast."

"Yeah, well, I've also never felt you come on me. You get special treatment now." I walked back to her and braced my hands on either side of her shoulders, lowering my face to hers. "Eggs and toast work?"

She nodded, not trying to suppress her smile. Dipping down, I pressed a kiss to her lips, then grabbed her hand and tugged her out of bed.

"Come keep me company."

She linked her fingers with mine and followed me into the kitchen, still wearing my too-big sweatshirt, her legs bare. Through the two summers we'd been neighbors, I'd seen her countless times in less clothing than this—a tank top and shorts, or a swimsuit. But there was something so fucking hot about having so much of her covered by *my* clothes.

Tearing my eyes away from her, I headed to the fridge. "Scrambled okay?"

"Sure, I'm not picky."

She hopped up on the counter and sat silently, watching as I prepared breakfast. What struck me as weird was how...not weird this was between us. There was no awkward morning after. No uncomfortable bouts of silence. It was like it had always been between us—contentment and companionship—but now the cloud of sexual tension that had hung over us had re-formed into sexual *awareness*. I no longer had to wonder what sounds she made when she came. No longer had to wonder how long it'd take to get her off, how she liked to kiss, how she'd feel under my fingers. I knew—not enough…not nearly enough. But still, I knew.

I desperately wanted to spend all our time learning every inch of her body, but there were things we couldn't avoid anymore—things we needed to discuss. As much as I didn't want to burst this bubble we were in, as much as I wanted to forget exactly what I'd seen last night when she'd run from that house, I couldn't. And I needed to know for certain what was going on. I needed my suspicions confirmed or put to rest once and for all.

After handing her the plate of eggs, I poured us each a glass of orange juice, letting her dig in before I dropped the bomb.

"When are we going to talk about what happened last night?"

She paused with her fork in midair, her eyes shooting to mine. "I was sort of hoping we could skip it."

I set my plate next to her on the counter and reached out, tracing the bottom curve of her lip. "You know we can't."

Bringing her uneaten forkful to her plate, she

pushed the eggs around. "I don't tell anyone…this. Ever."

"Does it have to do with what you said in there?" I asked, gesturing to the bedroom. "When you said you were attracted to me, but it was never an option?"

"I…" She bit her lip then sighed. "Yeah, it does."

I moved to stand between her legs, resting my hands on her thighs. "You know you can tell me anything, right? It won't change how I feel about you."

She nodded, set her plate down, and finally met my eyes. Her face was drawn, her expression nearly pained as she took a deep breath and squared her shoulders. "Do you know what an escort is?"

My stomach dropped, the pieces of the puzzle all sliding into place. My suspicions proved. I swallowed through the tightness in my throat. "Of course I know what it is."

She nodded, glancing toward the living room. Avoiding my eyes again as she said, "So you know not all escorts have sex with clients, right?"

"Yeah, Lo." I squeezed her thighs to try to reassure her with my touch that I'd accept whatever it was she had to tell me. That I wouldn't judge her for what had gone on.

For long moments, she stared into the other room. When she finally looked back at me, there was no smile. No glint in her eyes. No dimple. No Lola.

"I started off in the…standard role. Dates, money—" She paused, scrunching her nose as if the word she was looking for somehow tasted bad. She bit down on her bottom lip, gnawing for a second before taking a deep breath. "Sex. Dates, money, and sex. Totally what people expect. But at some point, the owner of the company realized the fact that I look young, that I was so short, even, was a more profitable asset."

"Jesus, you're talking about yourself like you're a commodity, Lo. You're a fucking *person*."

Her eyes shone with wetness, and a pained expression ghosted across her face. "Not always. When I'm her—when I'm Lolita—I'm something for sale. I fulfill a need for a client that usually revolves around…nonsexual yet intimate acts."

I could barely process what she was saying— referring to herself as something for sale. Like she was a product and not a human being. I hated it, hated everything about it. But it was her life, her choice— my gut churned at the possibility that it hadn't been. To be sure, I asked, "And last night… Last night was…a job?"

"Yes. He was a client of mine, one I've seen regularly for almost two years." She frowned as she played with the hem of the sweatshirt she wore, her eyes downcast. "One I hope never to see again."

Something in the tone of her voice sparked my instincts, made my stomach clench and my throat tight. "Did he do something to you? Did he hurt you?" If that fucker did anything to her—laid a hand on her without her consent… "I don't have jurisdiction off the island, but I've got a few buddies over there. I can make a call."

She started shaking her head before I could even get all the words out, placing a hand on my arm as if to calm me. "That's not necessary. He didn't do anything to me. When you got there, when you saw me running out, that was all on me. He never crossed a line—I couldn't go through with the appointment. It was my fault."

"That's *bullshit*, Lo. If you don't want to do something, it's your right to walk away. You don't owe your body to anyone. Ever."

She stared at me, the look on her face nearly enough to kill me. The lack of life in her eyes downright scary. "Unless they pay me for it."

I didn't give a single flying fuck if they gave her fifty gold bricks. She didn't owe anyone anything if she didn't want to give it. Jaw clenched, fists balled up against her thighs, I said, "Even then."

"Connor, I had a job to do. An appointment with a man who relies on me to act a certain way and trusts me to keep his secrets. Yes, I had a right to tell him no, but I also had a responsibility as a professional to make sure he had someone there to fulfill my role or to follow through with the deal myself. And I couldn't." She raised her hand and rested it against my cheek. "I couldn't go through with it because I couldn't get you off my mind."

I turned my head to press a kiss on her palm. "Why now? Why, after all this time?"

"I don't know. My job…it changed me. Made me not trust people. Made me feel disconnected from everyone because I had to keep my secrets." She dropped her hand from my face and set it on top of mine where it rested on her thigh. "My life was already hard because of my family going back to Ecuador after I graduated high school. Living with the lies and knowing how strange some men could get only made me pull inside myself further." She shrugged, a smile lifting up one side of her mouth. "But you never let me hide. You barged into my life and stayed there, and I adore you for it. You've always been special to me." She hooked her legs around my hips, tugging me closer. Pressing up against me. "I never wanted to bring that life into ours."

I wrapped my arms around her, slipping my hands under the sweatshirt and settling them against her back. She sighed, melting into my touch. "You know this doesn't change anything, right? I promised you whatever you had to tell me wouldn't change my feelings, and it hasn't."

She cocked her head to the side, her eyebrows rising. "So you're fine with the fact that men paid me to fulfill their fantasies? Sometimes sexually?"

Fuck no, I wasn't. Even a little. But I wasn't so much of an asshole to tell her what she could and couldn't do with her life. I knew enough about her situation to know she didn't have it easy, that she didn't come from a well-off family who could help put her through college. That she needed to do that on her own—by whatever means. I could look past a lot if it was her choice. But if it wasn't? "And did they always have your consent? Did anyone…did they take—"

"Never. Other than the guy last week, no one has ever gotten more out of hand than I expected them to. I may not have wanted to do all the things I've done, but I wanted the cash I earned doing them because I needed a job, and the money was easy. I'm not some sad, put-upon girl who got swept up. I made the choice to work in a particular field, and I can't put that on anyone else's shoulders."

I hated it. Hated that it was her job, that she'd gotten into it not because she'd *wanted* to but because she *had* to—for money. Hated every single thing about the circumstances. But it didn't change anything. She was still Lo to me. And yet… "I'm not going to lie to you—I can't stand the thought of you with them."

She bit her lip again, looking at me with those wide eyes of hers. Imploring me with her words. "Then stop thinking about them."

I shook my head. "It's not that easy. Every time I close my eyes—"

"Stop." She pushed against my chest to get me to step back, then slid off the counter. "They don't matter. Whether I did those things just to do them or for money, it has nothing to do with us. And last night was it—the end of Lolita—the last appointment I'll accept. I can't keep doing what I have been. Not with how I feel about myself." Pressing close, she tucked her fingers into the waistband of my sweat pants, staring up at me with eyes bright and full of longing. "Not with how I feel about you."

I breathed for what felt like the first time since she'd started telling me everything, my chest loosening with relief. No more working jobs she didn't want to.

No more putting herself at risk. Gripping her hips, I held her close. "And how's that?"

Walking backward, she tugged me along with her hands pulling the drawstrings at my waist, a smile tipping up the corners of her lips. "Let me show you."

She didn't stop until she was in my bathroom. Then she turned on the water and came over to me, her hands going straight to my waistband. And as much I wanted to be naked with her, to feel her skin under my hands, I needed to make sure it was her choice.

I stilled her hands before she could pull off my sweats. "Be sure, beautiful. Be sure."

She looked up at me, then removed her hands from under mine and went straight to the hem of the sweatshirt. And then she tugged it off and tossed it to the side. "I've been sure for a long time. Are you?"

chapter six

LOLA

I WAITED ON tenterhooks, needing his answer. His admission. When he finally groaned a, "Fuck yes, I'm sure," I nearly sagged with relief. This was it, us, something we'd both been wanting, apparently. Probably for months…maybe, like me, for the two years since we'd met. I was done waiting.

Without another delay, I pushed his sweat pants down his legs, baring him to me. Both of us naked for the first time. And he was beautiful—so much paler than I was, with freckles across his chest and hair dusting his body. I wanted to run my hands all over him, wanted to follow those trails with my lips. But first…

"Let me wash you," I whispered, unable to keep my hands off his skin.

He tugged me closer, looming over me. "I'd love

nothing more than to have your hands on me. But I want to take care of you. Let me."

No one had even *attempted* to take care of me in years. No one but Connor. Even as friends, he'd cared. Hell, as strangers, he'd ingrained himself into my world and become that overprotective presence that I'd longed to spend more time with. And there we were, naked and alone, about to embark on some sort of physical journey together, and he was still trying to put me first. My God, if I loved the man any more, I'd fall at his feet and beg him to be mine.

Luckily, I didn't have to.

I pressed my lips to his and pulled him with me into the shower, closing the curtain behind us once we were in the tub. This was our new start, our baptism into something more than friendship, more than secrets and lies between us. This was our rebirth. I took a moment simply to look at him, to try to implore with my eyes how important this moment was. How meaningful. And when I felt comfortable he understood, when the expression on his face was as loving and soft as I'd ever dreamed it could be, I smiled.

"That's my favorite smile," he said, his voice soft, his fingers brushing over my cheek. And then, even though this had been my plan, he began to wash me.

There was something so meaningful about that moment, something beyond sex or sensuality. There was a coming together, a feeling of intimacy that hadn't been there before. Even when I'd straddled his hips, even when he came while on top of me— nothing compared to this.

With gentle hands, he pulled my hair back and wet it from the crown. He brushed his fingers across my neck, his body pressing into my side as he cupped his hand and pulled the water all the way to the ends. Then he washed it, and that brought sensations I'd never experienced. Strong fingers ran through my hair, gentle in their motions. Loving, almost. I closed my eyes and surrendered to the feeling, letting Connor do as he needed. Giving myself to him in that moment.

When my hair was clean, he let his hands swoop lower, spreading soap and suds along my shoulders and down my back. Rubbing me. Cleansing me. His breaths matched mine, his need something palpable in the air around us. How such a simple act could be so sensual, I had no idea. But I liked it. No, I loved it.

When I was clean, Connor pressed against my back, sliding his hands around the front of my hips. Pulling me close and trapping his hard cock between us.

"I hate that they had their hands on you." He kissed my neck softly, gentle in ways I never knew he could be.

And his words… I understood that statement better than he could have thought. I hated that I'd *let* them have their hands on me, that I'd potentially shadowed my future with the decisions in my past. The idea that I could have missed out on something as wonderful as that moment in the shower with Connor—that I could have lost him completely—was heartbreaking and the sort of reality check I needed.

Wanting to give him as much care as he showed me, I turned in his arms, rising onto the balls of my feet to reach for him. To brush my lips against his. To press our bodies together for one moment under the falling water. We both hated that I'd been touched, but we could fix that. We could start anew. We could start again with something more, something meaningful. Something that was just us.

"We'll wash them away," I whispered before placing one last kiss on his lips. "We'll wash them all away and start fresh. Just you and me."

Connor stared at me for a long time, holding me close. Not moving except to raise his hands, to cup my face. He held me like I was precious, like I was something special. Something I'd never experienced. And when he finally spoke, when he rocked us closer together and used his fingers to tuck my wet hair behind my ears, he gave me the one response I needed.

"Okay."

All the stress I'd been carrying disappeared, and the weight of my worry evaporated. Okay was enough. Okay was perfect. And it was time I let him know that.

"Duck," I said, pulling away from his body enough so I could pour shampoo into my hand. Connor didn't even blink at my command, bending at the waist and holding on to my hips as he did. The man had a thing for keeping me close. For keeping us connected. And I loved it.

I scrubbed through his hair, massaging his scalp and neck on every pass. Leaning closer with every touch. He held still for me, though his hands kept moving. Kept pulling me closer. Kept kneading my flesh. His touch was killing me, making me need. Making me want things I wasn't sure how to ask for.

"Done." I inched back when I was finished, grabbing his bar of soap with shaking hands so I could cleanse him. And I did—I scrubbed him from the tops of his shoulders to the tips of his toes. Worked my hands over every inch of skin, over parts that made him jump and squirm and parts that made him groan. He was so hard the whole time, his cock practically bouncing as he followed my movements. I wanted to touch it, taste it, make him come again…wanted to take him in my mouth and feel his hands in my hair as I swallowed around him. I even reached for him at one point, wrapped my hand around the base of him and stroked him from root to tip.

Connor, though, had other plans.

"Come here, Lo." He lifted me to my feet, letting me brush his body with mine. Pulling me until I stood before him, still under the shower spray. Still naked. Still needy.

Connor stared down at me for a long moment, his hands endlessly sliding over my flesh. Seeking something. Searching for what, I had no idea. But on one pass, he didn't come back up when he reached my thighs. No, he kept going, dropping his entire body to his knees right there in the shower so he could kiss and nibble at my tummy. At my hip bone. At my—

"Connor." I grabbed his hair as he ran his nose along the front of my slit. As he moved as if to do something I had never been the recipient of.

"This okay?" His grumbly, deep voice made me tremble, and I nearly fell back against the wall because of it. Connor simply followed me, keeping up his pressure. His teasing. Swiping his tongue along the very top of me as if waiting for me to give him permission to move lower.

Oh God, did I want him to move lower. "I've never... I don't know..."

His eyes turned hungry, a sort of feral gleam in them as they darted up to meet mine. A sexy-as-fuck sort of gleam. "No one's ever licked your pussy?"

That word on his lips made said pussy quiver. I shook my head, too embarrassed to speak. Too turned on to lie. I'd seen all sorts of things—done all sorts of things—but intimacy like that? Having someone to be willing to do *that* to me? Never.

Apparently, my time as a cunnilingus virgin was coming to a close.

Connor ran his nose over me again, reaching out his tongue to flick across my flesh. Delving deeper, lower, teasing me as he pulled my hips toward him. I gasped and jerked, wet already from his touch. Soaked, really. Aching for him in ways no one had ever made me feel before.

Connor took his time, though. He was a caretaker, after all. He lifted one leg and washed my foot, kissing the top of it before moving his lips up to my knee. Higher yet, to the fleshiest part of my thigh.

I was a trembling mess, one hand locked in his hair, the other pressed flat against the wall behind me as he rose on his knees to press his face between my legs.

But he didn't.

Before he could reach where I so wanted him to be, he moved on to the next foot, lifting me right off the ground and supporting me as I leaned against the shower wall. His touches were soft, his kisses gentle even as he used his strength to hold me up. I could barely breathe, could hardly stand to watch him progress up my thighs, but I had to. The image was too perfect, the picture something I would never forget. His shoulders flexed with every kiss, his grip growing tighter as he pulled my thighs apart. And this time, when he reached the top of my thigh, when he kissed so high, his cheek brushed against my pussy, he didn't stop.

And he wasn't gentle.

Connor dove in with the appetite of a starving man, his tongue and lips seeking and finding my clit on their first pass. On the first swipe that set my entire body on fire. I gasped and slammed my hands against the shower wall, hanging on, staring down at the amazing man between my legs. How could he do that? How did he know how to make me feel so good? How was he strong enough to hold me up and still press his mouth against me and—

"Oh God, Connor." I writhed against his face, unable to hold still, seeking more no matter how much he gave. Falling deeper into my orgasm spiral with every swipe, every suck. Every second that he worked me over. He flicked and licked, he spread me with his thumbs and suckled, he even ran his teeth along me. But when he hummed? When the combination of the stubble brushing against my thighs and the vibration of his lips on my clit met?

Done.

I came with a short yelp, rolling my body forward as if to protect myself from the pleasure burning within. Every twitch enhanced the sensations, every brush of Connor's skin against mine intensified the deep throb of completion. Of connection. Connor set my feet back on the ground and held me up, letting that pleasure roll through at its own pace, keeping one hand between my legs to tease out every ounce. Every drop. Every shake and tremor.

"I don't—" I moaned as another tremble shot over me. "I have no idea how you do that."

"Does that mean I did okay for your first time?" The cocky grin he shot up at me should have been annoying, but how could it be? The man had practically made me forget my name.

I didn't even try to answer him with anything more than a groan. I also didn't try to move—I was pretty sure my legs had stopped working. Connor, luckily, seemed to know exactly what to do. He shut off the water and picked me up, carrying me out of the tub. I clung to his shoulders, curling around him, wanting so much more of his touch. His warmth. Like the caregiver he was, he set me on the rug and grabbed a towel to dry me off. He even squeezed the water out of my hair. And then, with a lustful look in his eyes and a sexual tension that seemed to vibrate around him, he picked me up.

And he carried me to bed.

chapter seven

CONNOR

I'D THOUGHT ABOUT this moment more than I'd ever admit. Had dreamt about it, fantasized about it when I got myself off. Stroked myself to the imagined taste of her…to the sound of her moans in my head. And now, as she lay on my bed, her towel coming loose and falling open to expose her body, I no longer had to wonder. I knew intimately the noises she made when she came. I knew the taste of her pussy, how wet she got, how tight she was. And every bit of it was even better than my dreams, so I was going to enjoy every goddamn second of this.

Everyday Lola was gorgeous in her uniform of yoga pants and hoodies. Last night, Sleepy Lola had made my cock ache while lying there in only my sweatshirt. Naked Lola? She took my goddamn breath away. She was…exquisite. A tiny waist gave way to the subtle flare of hips, small breasts tipped with dark nipples just begging for my mouth. I wanted nothing more than to swoop down and feel them on my tongue.

But before I allowed myself to indulge, I had to be sure that she still wanted this. That she wanted everything. It was one thing to let me go down on her in the shower. Another thing entirely to allow me every inch of her body. And after everything she'd told me earlier, I had to make sure she knew the choice was one hundred percent hers.

"How much will you give me, beautiful?" I caged her in on the bed, careful to keep our bodies from touching, and brushed a kiss below her ear. "How much will you let me have?"

She arched her back, seeking me out. Reaching for me as she whispered, "Everything. Take it all."

That was all I needed to hear. Even though I'd already kissed every inch of her body in the shower, had felt her come on my tongue, I had the overwhelming urge to…*love* her. Over and over again. With my body and my words and my actions. So I did. I brushed openmouthed kisses across her collarbones, between the valley of her breasts, sucked their tips into my mouth. Gave love bites to the small curve of her stomach. Swiped my fingers through her slit, then followed behind with my tongue. I taunted her clit with fluttering touches followed by harsh suction, listening the entire time to her body, studying her reactions. Learning everything she had to teach me about what she loved.

She didn't disappoint.

Moans spilled from her lips as she arched against the bed, her fingers delving in my hair. Tugging me closer then pushing me away before yanking me back. I filled my hands with her ass and lifted her closer to my mouth, relishing in the fact that I was the only one who'd ever had her like this. The only one who knew the taste of her pussy, the pulse of her clit on my tongue. It was something only we shared.

Pulling away, I worked circles around her clit with my thumb, pressing a kiss to her inner thigh. I glanced up at her, seeing her watching me with hooded eyes. "I love that I'm the only one who's swallowed your come."

She reached out, running her fingers down my jaw. "You'll always be the only one."

With a smile, I dove in, working her slow and sweet, fast and hard. Taking her up and over the edge again. And again. And again. I lost count of how many times she came, her body arching under me, tits filling my palms, heels digging into my shoulders. My cock was so hard it ached, precome leaking from the tip, but I could spend all night with my face between her legs, never getting relief, and still die a happy man.

After another orgasm, she finally pushed me away, her panting breaths mixed with contented sighs. "Connor...want you inside me."

I wanted that, too. Desperately. Wanted to feel what it'd be like to sink into her petite body, feel her snug little pussy wrapped all around me. I kissed her inner thigh, sinking my teeth in just enough to make her jump. Then I made my way up her body before snagging a condom from the nightstand and rolling it down my length.

"You gonna come all over my cock like you did my tongue?"

"Yes. God, yes. Please."

Hands braced on either side of her shoulders, I leaned down and pressed my mouth to hers. Swept my tongue between her lips. Swallowed her moan. She writhed under me, wrapping her arms around my shoulders as she tugged me down.

Allowing our lips to brush with each word, I said, "You feel so good under me."

She sighed into my mouth, hooking her legs around my hips and urging me closer with her heels pressed into my ass. I wanted nothing more than to slide into her, fill her completely, but I'd been thinking about this for so long, had been fantasizing about it daily, that I wanted to memorize every second of it. How she stared up at me, her fingers restless on my shoulders. How she rolled her hips up toward me, grinding her hungry little clit against the head of my cock. How she tried to pull me down, force me even closer, as if we weren't already lined up from head to toe. But what I would think about over and over again, what would keep me company on nights when she couldn't, was how her eyelids fluttered shut, how she whispered my name as I finally sank deep inside.

"*Jesus*," I groaned, eyes closing before I snapped them open, wanting to watch her face as she took my cock for the first time. Goddamn, she was tiny.

Everywhere. And so fucking wet. I rocked back and forth, working myself in as she stretched around me. Her pussy gripped me like a vise, her walls already pulsing as I settled fully inside her.

"Connor…" She stared up at me, her mouth open, eyes wide. Like she couldn't believe anything could feel this good. Like she couldn't believe pleasure like this even existed.

"I know, beautiful." I kissed her, soft and sweet, our chests pressing together, then I pulled back and thrust deep, driving her up toward the headboard. She gasped, then groaned, tilting her head back and exposing her neck to me, pushing her tits against my chest. "You feel so good. So fucking good."

I pressed my forehead to her neck and brushed a kiss against her collarbone. Whispered her name as I filled her over and over again. Her nearly nonstop moans punctuated by the slap of our bodies coming together was the best sound I'd ever heard. It was only eclipsed when she'd say my name in that breathy, awed way she did. I wanted to hear it every goddamn day—every goddamn *hour*.

"You have any idea how long I've wanted you like this? How many times I've thought about this exact thing?"

She stilled under me, her breath catching. Then she whispered, "Tell me."

"Since day fucking one." I pushed deep, grinding the base of my cock right against her clit. "I've thought of a hundred different ways to make you come— some of them on my fingers or my tongue—but this was always my favorite. Feeling you pulse around my cock—ah, shit. Just like that."

She dropped her legs open, letting me push even deeper. "Connor, Connor…"

"That's it. Come on, sweet girl. Let me feel you." I scraped my teeth against her neck as she bowed off the bed and dug her fingernails into my shoulders, a loud moan spilling from her lips. And then she was coming, her pussy pulsing around me, and it was all I needed to let go.

"Lo…*Jesus*…"

Groaning, I buried my face in her neck as I came, loving how she whispered my name over and over again as I did, her heels pressed into my ass, holding me deep inside her. For long moments, I lay boneless on top of her, trying to catch my breath, while she traced soft paths up and down the length of my back. I wanted nothing more than to stay like this, pressed up against her…as close as we could possibly get, but logistics got in the way.

With a kiss to her neck, I pulled back, only to meet resistance as she squeezed me closer.

She shook her head, nuzzling her face into my neck, breathing me in just like I'd done to her. Against my skin, she said, "Not yet."

I smiled and pressed a kiss to her temple. "I promise I'll be right back."

She relinquished her hold with a pout, and I brushed a kiss across that puffed-out bottom lip, nipping at it before heading to the bathroom to dispose of the condom. Once I made my way back to the bedroom, I used her long-forgotten towel to get her cleaned up, then tossed it to the side and climbed in next to her.

Curling against her, I slipped an arm around her waist and tugged her back to my chest. I relished the soft hum she gave, how she shimmied her ass right up against me, like she was trying to get closer. Rubbing small circles on her stomach with my thumb, I kissed the nape of her neck before inhaling deeply. Loving that my sheets now smelled like us.

"We can't spend all day in bed…" Lola whispered.

"I don't know. I'm not on duty until tonight, which means we *can* spend all day in bed." I reached up and cupped one of her breasts, rubbing my thumb over her nipple until it hardened under my touch. "Unless that doesn't sound appealing to you…"

"It sounds like my own personal sort of heaven, to be honest."

Mine too.

chapter eight

LOLA

MY CAR SAT outside the four-plex, unused. My rosary beads rested in a bowl by the front door, waiting for me to need them. To take them to the sanctuary for prayer. I didn't go. I had become a bit of a recluse, afraid even to look at my mail or answer my phone. It hadn't taken long for that anxiety to manifest—the first time Rumor had called after I'd run out of my John's house, my heart rate had spiked. The first time I'd received a letter from school about a tuition payment due, my hands had gone clammy. The two were definitely linked together, and both were things I needed to get a handle on.

It was time to be an adult and deal with the world around me.

My apartment was dark and cold when I opened the door. I'd been staying at Connor's for the past week. Sure, I'd come down here to grab my stuff, but he was overly concerned about the locks not being strong enough, so he always came with me. When he worked, I hung out in his apartment studying, watching my shows, cooking for him—I loved cooking for him. When he was home, we were together. There was usually no need to be down in what was technically my apartment. No need to spend time in the space I paid for but didn't use.

And yet, I couldn't hide away any longer.

I shut the door behind me and headed straight for my little desk against the kitchen wall. It had always been warmest there, so I'd set up my office-slash-studying area in the awkward spot. Connor used to joke about knocking over my computer when he was headed for the bathroom, a thought that made me smile. But I couldn't get distracted. Connor would be home from work soon, and I had things to do.

I dialed the number I knew by heart, the same one I'd been ignoring for days. The same one I knew I should have called the night I'd bailed on my appointment. The night I'd decided to quit my job.

"You'd better have a good explanation for not answering my calls, bitch."

I huffed a laugh, able to picture Rumor's scowl. She'd be at her desk in her house, the one very few girls ever got to see. Knowing her, she was wearing something super sexy and expensive, something tailored to every curve. And red. She always wore red.

"Hey, Rumor. I know you're probably really pissed at me—"

"Hold up, Lola. Pissed doesn't begin to describe it." She paused, the soft thump of what was probably a door closing my only indicator of what she was doing. "You run away crying from an appointment, a fact which the goddamn John had to tell me because you refused to answer your phone. You also get picked up by some guy in front of that John's house, tucked into a car, and driven away—again, something the John had to tell me. Do you have any fucking idea how worried I've been? I had Knox go to your apartment to see if you were alive. He said the place looked as if no one was living there anymore. So, no, sweetcheeks. Pissed doesn't even begin to describe what I am right now."

Oh God. She'd sent Knox. If Connor had seen him, if he'd run into the hulking, giant of a man Rumor used as her personal security force, he'd never let me out of his sight.

"I'm sorry," I whispered, feeling small and young at her chastisement. Knowing I deserved it.

"I accept your apology. Now, where the fuck have you been?"

"Safe. On the island, but not really at home. Rumor, that night…" I closed my eyes, remembering the sense of drowning. The way I couldn't stand to be in that costume. The way thoughts of Connor had invaded my mind. "I'd just had enough. I didn't want to do the job anymore."

There was quiet from the other end, the only sound Rumor breathing. And then she sighed. "Aw, kid. I get that. I just wish you would have called me or answered your phone. You know my rules—you don't have to do anything you don't want to, and no one works for me against their will."

"I know. And I should have answered you. It's just been… I mean, after Connor picked me up—"

"Hang on," she interjected, suddenly sounding almost excited. "That was Connor who picked you up? The hottie neighbor you've been crushing on practically since birth?"

I might have told her about Connor a time or two. Okay, every day. Though I'd never told her what he did for a living. She probably wouldn't have been as excited if she knew. "Yeah. We're sort of a…a thing now."

"Does he know?" Three words. That was all she said, but the meaning behind it was clear. Did he know what I did for a living? Did he know how I sold myself? Did he know some people would never *not* see me as a whore?

"He knows." I bit my lip, picturing Connor as he thrust into me that morning. Remembering the smile on his face and the gentleness of his hands. The filthy words he'd used to make sure I knew I was his. "He cares about me anyway."

"As he damn well should. You're a dish." She hummed a little as the sound of papers being moved crept over the line. "So I'm going to assume you're retiring, yes?"

That was an easy one. "Yes. Definitely."

"Not gonna lie, kid—I'm sad to see you go, but I understand. I'll send Knox over your way in a few.

He's going to have some papers for you to sign—standard stuff, nothing to worry about."

I glanced at the clock. "Connor will be home in about an hour, and I don't want—"

"Understood. He'll be quick and discreet. You…" She paused again, and this time when her voice came back through the line, business Rumor was gone and in her place was the woman I'd told my life story to. The one who'd given me ice cream and taken care of me the first time I'd had a John treat me like dirt. The woman who worried about the girls working for her more than she ever let on. "You go grab your happily ever after, okay? Grab it tight and never let it go."

My eyes burned as I whispered, "I will."

"Good girl. Knox will be there in twenty."

I sat on the floor staring at my phone, missing my connection to Rumor already. She'd been such a force in my life these past couple of years, such a strong figure to follow. I was oddly going to miss her.

Fifteen minutes had passed when the knock at the door came. A quick look out the peephole confirmed my assumption, and I opened it to find Knox standing in my hallway. Or rather, blocking the hallway for anyone who might try to move past him.

"Miss Rumor requires your signature." He handed me a flat envelope with a black and red symbol on the top. The same sort of envelope I'd received when I'd signed on to work for her.

I took the packet of documents and headed to the kitchen counter, grabbing a pen as I passed my desk. Everything looked on the up-and-up. Termination of employment, exit interview, and nondisclosure agreements, mostly. No naming names, no tell-all books, no discussing what escort jobs were like in public settings, never discussing who Rumor was or what her business did. For all the world, we'd worked as upscale escorts, offering temporary companionship to men who could afford us. The sex…well, that had been off the books. And Rumor didn't exist.

I signed everything I needed to, tucking the papers back into the envelope when I was done. For the last time, I ran my finger over Rumor's symbol—a bright red swirl of a bird, a phoenix, she'd told me once. Hopefully, it was my turn to rise from the ashes like she had.

"Here you go," I said to Knox as I handed the envelope back to him. "Please tell Rumor I'm going to miss her."

He nodded. "I'm sure she feels the same, Miss Lola."

I followed him to the door as he turned to leave, but just before he stepped outside, he pulled another envelope from his pocket. This one smaller. And red.

"Miss Rumor would like to congratulate you on your college graduation."

I stared at the envelope, my brow tight. "I haven't graduated yet."

He tucked the envelope in my hands and smiled… sort of. "But you will, and Miss Rumor figured you wouldn't mind if she sent your gift early. Good luck, Lola."

I stood in my open doorway and stared after him for a good few seconds, watching the outer door close behind him. Watching a chapter of my life close right before my eyes. The red envelope burned my palm, though, and I had to open it. I had to know what she'd done.

I sliced through the top with my finger, tearing the beautiful paper easily. Inside…well, inside was my salvation.

Cash.

Thousands of dollars of cash.

A quick flip through the hundred-dollar bills told me I had at least ten thousand dollars. And at the back, at the bottom of the pile of green, was a small red card with a mere ten words on it.

Be careful—judgment lingers—but don't let that stop you.

She didn't even sign her name, but she didn't need to. Only Rumor would do something so kind, would remind me of the nature of the business while pushing me to do what I wanted anyway. Only Rumor—

"Lo? What are you doing down here, beautiful?" Connor appeared in the doorway, his heavy coat still zipped over his dark blue uniform, his brow drawn. "And why the fuck is the door wide open?" He stalked through the little apartment, looking in every closet and behind every door. Searching for a threat, of course. When he was finished, he grabbed my arms and pulled me against him. Surrounded me with his security and his body once more. "Are you okay?"

I wasn't sure how to speak. How to tell him. Didn't know how to put into words how excited I was. Rumor had just thrown me a lifeline, one that could keep me on the island and in school for months. One that made me feel financially secure enough to take my time finding a new job. Rumor had just made me the happiest girl on earth.

And I wanted Connor to feel the same way.

"I missed you," I said, as I tossed the envelope onto the table behind him. No sense explaining that right off the bat, not when he was already so concerned. Not when we had something to celebrate.

"I missed you, too, but that doesn't answer—"

He didn't get to finish his sentence because I yanked him down and pressed my mouth to his. It took him a second to respond, but once he did, he took over. Grabbing my ass, pulling me against him, groaning into a deepening kiss as he slid his tongue against mine.

"Want you," I said when we broke apart. And my God, did I. He looked so amazing in that uniform with his cheeks pink from being out in the cold. So delicious.

I tugged him toward the couch, unbuckling his belt as we moved. There was no use waiting—I was wet for him, had been since the moment he walked in. I just had to get him naked.

Connor caught up with me quickly. He shrugged off his coat, his cold hands then moving to lift the shirt I was wearing. Stumbling, rough and greedy with our hands, we stripped each other as best we could. My need had become a wild thing, an energy all its own. A desire I couldn't restrain. When we reached the couch, I shoved him down and crawled on top of his legs, unable to wait a second more than I absolutely had to. This was my show, my turn, my happiness to give. My relief to share.

"What's going on with you?" Connor asked, staring up at me, giving me that lazy sort of smile that made my heart flutter for him. His shirt was half unbuttoned, his white undershirt hiding his chest from me. Still, I ran my hands over the fabric, pressing hard, massaging. Needing to touch him.

"I got good news today." I reached down to where his pants lay on the floor and pulled a condom from his wallet. He'd said he didn't need to carry them anymore since we stayed home so much—whether he stashed them in his wallet or in the drawer next to the bed, he didn't see how it mattered. I'd reminded him we could have sex wherever we wanted if he had one with him. That had convinced him to keep one on him at all times, which was coming in handy.

Connor held on to my hips as I sheathed his cock, as I rocked over his thigh. He moaned and grabbed for me, and I followed his tug, making sure to run my fingers over his balls as I climbed up the length of his body. His groan was deep, his eyes hooded and lust-filled, and I was ready for him. Always. Every time.

"Lo," he whispered as I moved up and held the base of his cock.

"Be with me, Connor. Just be with me."

When he nodded, I slid down, taking him inside me, joining us together. Finally. There was something so tension-filled about those first moments together, so restrained but wild. He'd rock just enough to slide deep inside me, and I'd hang on to whatever part of him I could grab. Adjusting to him, taking him in. Readying myself for what was to come. He was huge, my Connor. Long and thick in a way that both smarted and felt so good. And the man knew how to move, knew how to use more than his hard cock to work my body over.

With a groan, Connor thrust up, his hands on my hips and holding me in place. His cock pushing deeper inside of me. So deep, I never wanted him to leave. Never wanted him to move, but that wouldn't happen. Didn't happen. The man worked for every ounce of my pleasure and his, rolling his hips, pushing up with his legs, using his arms to move my body on him. He was a goddamned fucking machine, and I was the lucky girl who got to handle him every day.

Our sex wasn't slow or sweet; it wasn't rough, though, either. It was messy and slightly awkward on such a small couch, but it was us. He gave me everything he had, always so considerate and attentive in his affections. Always so present when we were together. I tried to return that to him, to earn his care with my own. I rode him hard, rocking and bouncing and leaning back so I could take as much of his cock as possible. Working my hips and squeezing the muscles inside to give him everything I had. Everything he needed.

But Connor never just took. No. He was a giver, especially in our sex life. Connor played with my tits, my clit, rubbing my legs, spreading my pussy so he could watch me take all of him. He muttered obscene things about my body—how wet I was for him, how swollen and tight. How he loved watching my tits bounce, how he wanted to fuck me from behind so he could see my ass turn red from his hands on me. He was so totally in the moment, so beyond noticing anything other than the two of us, and that was all because of me. Because of us. Because of our connection. My filthy fucking savior.

And when I came, when I called his name as I clenched around his cock, I knew there would never be anyone else for me. No man could ever make me feel as beautiful and as cared for as Connor did; no other person could ever make me feel so loved. He was my knight in shining armor, my prince, and my best friend. I certainly didn't deserve him, but I was going to do my best to earn him.

With one final swerve of my hips and an arch off the couch from him, Connor groaned and finally surrendered to his own orgasm. He held me close as his body went rigid under mine, pulling me down so we had more contact. Thrusting deep one last time as he practically growled through his release.

As his entire body seemed to seek out ways to touch mine.

As he whispered my name like a chant.

Perfect…and mine.

chapter nine

CONNOR

LOLA LAY BONELESS on my chest, her panting breaths matching mine as I trailed my fingers up and down the length of her back. Jesus, I could get used to this, coming home and being met with my girl ready to fuck, pouncing on me as soon as I walked through the door. Except for one problem: we weren't at home—or where I'd started to think of as home, anyway.

She'd been staying with me since the night I'd found her on the mainland, and I'd enjoyed every single second of it. I loved seeing her face when I walked through the door after a long shift. Loved that she'd always greet me with a bright smile, that dimple popping out. Loved that she'd sometimes greet me with that smile *and* one of her delicious as hell meals—like she wanted to take care of me. Loved holding her as we fell asleep. Loved waking to her head nestled on my chest, her hand resting on my stomach, legs entangled with mine. Like she couldn't quite get close enough—a sentiment I understood.

But she hadn't greeted me at my place.

Walking into the four-plex after my shift and seeing her door wide open had almost sent me into cardiac arrest, my mind going immediately back to that evening in the alley, pulling that asshole off her. The bone-deep fear for her safety had nearly choked me. And then she'd been standing there, happy and glowing, and that panic had eased somewhat. Anything that could make my girl smile like that couldn't be all bad.

The unease was back, though. Did she come down here every day while I was at work? The thought of her here without me when I hadn't yet been able to replace her locks killed me. Between work and spending ninety percent of the remaining time inside Lola, I hadn't made it a priority. And now here she was, in her poorly secured apartment, all because I hadn't gotten my shit together to fix it for her. Having her down here—especially when I wasn't with her to do a sweep of the place first—made me twitchy as fuck given her history.

Still, she was safe now. In my arms.

I pressed a kiss against her forehead. "Not that I'm complaining, but what was that all about?"

Her cheek lifted against my chest, her smile so bright I could actually feel it. "I got good news today. I figured I could share my joy."

I laughed, reaching down to get a handful of her bare ass and squeezing. "You definitely shared it. But as distracting as your body is, don't think I've forgotten about the fact that you were down here with the door wide open."

She lifted her head, brought her hands to my chest, and settled her chin on top of them. Her smile dimming the tiniest bit.

Reaching out, I brushed a strand of hair back from her face. "You wanna tell me what the good news is?"

With a nod, she said, "My ex-boss sent me a graduation present. It's enough to pay my rent and tuition while I find a new job."

I frowned, the thought of her worrying about something as trivial as money squeezing my chest. Didn't she know by now that I'd do whatever I needed to—work overtime or get another job—to make sure she was happy? "Have you been worried about money?"

"Of course. Tuition is expensive, and rent needs to be paid every month. I don't want to be homeless."

"Beautiful, you know I'd never let you be homeless." Honestly, it was dumb as hell that she even had this place. She spent ninety-nine percent of her time in my apartment. And that was one percent less than it'd be if I had my way. The idea of being at work, knowing she was safe at home…*our* home? Knowing she'd actually *chosen* to make a home with me? I'd be the happiest asshole in the world. "You know there's a really easy solution to that, right?"

"Oh yeah? And what's that?"

"You're on a month-to-month lease, aren't you?"

"Yeah. I didn't want to deal with the whole background check thing just in case."

"Well, it's almost the end of the month. So maybe you terminate your lease." I smiled at the confusion showing on her face, how her brow drew tight, the corners of her mouth curving down. I reached up and smoothed the lines on her forehead. "Maybe you just move in with me instead."

She froze for a moment then her eyes went wide, and she pressed her lips together, like she was attempting to contain her smile. "Are you sure you're ready for that?"

Grabbing her ass with both hands, I hauled her up my body so I could kiss her. Here I thought I'd been completely transparent in my feelings for her, and she was worried it was too soon for me? Against her lips, I said, "If I had my way, you'd already be there."

She finally let that smile break free, her eyes sparkling with happiness. As quickly as it appeared, though, it fell from her face, seriousness taking over. "I'd want to pay my way. I won't be your charity case."

I had to work hard not to roll my eyes—I knew that wouldn't go over well. "You're not a burden, Lo. Could never be, even if you couldn't pay your way. I get why you want to—respect the hell out of you for it."

"Connor, I—"

I stopped her with a finger pressed to her lips. "But even if you can't, that doesn't matter to me. It doesn't."

"It should."

She still didn't get it. She was so independent. So fucking strong. Had worked hard to provide for herself for so long, and I loved that about her. Loved her determination and tenacity. Loved that she didn't *need* me to take care of her, but she *let* me. Allowed me that honor. It only made her stronger in my eyes. Only made me love her more.

And there was no getting around that…no avoiding it any longer. Sometime in the two years of our friendship, I'd fallen and I'd fallen hard. Now that she was mine? Forget it.

"It *doesn't* matter. Not with us. Not with *you*. There's not going to be some kind of tally between us. That's not how this is gonna work. I know you'd do the exact same thing for me, because that's how we are. I love you, and I'll always take care of what's mine, all right?"

She froze, her entire body stiffening. Shit, was it too soon? We'd only officially been together for like a week, but that didn't take into account the hundreds of days we'd shared prior to that. Didn't take into account hours upon hours we'd spent in each other's company, slowly falling in love during movies and shared pizza, tucked away in one of our apartments.

Before I could worry too much, she bit her bottom lip as a smile curved her mouth until she couldn't contain it. Until her dimple winked at me. When Lo was happy, her entire face lit up. In the time we'd known each other, I'd made it my mission to make her as happy as I could, whenever I could. And right then? She was beaming.

"All right," she said.

Returning her smile, I tugged her closer, nipping at her bottom lip. "All right? As in, yes, you'll move in?"

She laughed against my lips. "Yes, I'll move in with you."

With a groan, I took her mouth in a kiss, sliding my tongue against hers. Needing her closer than she was. She moaned into my mouth, grinding down on my already hard cock. I wanted nothing more than to slip inside her again, watch her as she rode me until she came all over me. Later. I'd just had her, so I could wait a couple hours to fuck her again. What I wanted right then was to take her out. Celebrate the step we were going to take.

I slowed my kisses, stilling her rocking hips with firm hands.

"Why are you stopping?" She pressed her lips out in a pout.

My laugh turned into a groan when she ground her pussy against me. "Believe me, I don't want to. But I think this calls for a celebration. How about we go out to El Placer? Margaritas and tortas and showing off my girl."

The smile dropped from her face as quickly as a light shutting off. "I don't know. What if…" She paused, looking down at her fingers as they traced circles on my chest before meeting my eyes. "I don't want to run into anyone."

I didn't know if her fear came from being recognized, or from being manhandled by a previous client. Didn't matter. I'd make sure she was safe.

"Lo…I'm not tossing you out to the wolves. I'd be with you, and you know I'd never let anything happen. You can't hide away for the rest of your life."

She blew out a breath and pushed back, resting her elbows on my chest. "I know, I'm just not ready yet. I don't want to leave our happy little bubble. And people come from the mainland for El Placer. There's more of a chance at someplace so touristy."

For a moment, I studied her, taking in the set of her shoulders, how the sparkle in her eyes had dimmed, the smile falling from her face. Hating that I'd taken away a bit of her happiness, but also knowing she couldn't spend the rest of her life tucked away in the apartment. Even if it was one we shared.

Relenting—for now—I said, "All right. Tonight, we'll get takeout instead. Watch *Weekend at Bernie's*. How's that sound?"

She smiled and pressed her lips to mine. "My favorite. You know my weaknesses."

I slipped my hand over her ass, trailing down between her legs until the wetness of her pussy met my fingers.

Groaning, she arched against me, lifting her ass and presenting herself to me. "See?"

"To be fair, I've always known tacos and comedies were your weaknesses. Figuring out having my tongue all over your pussy was another one is a fairly new development."

Her laughter turned into a moan when I slipped a finger inside her, then added another. She rocked against me, thrusting back while I fucked her with my fingers, rubbing her clit against the head of my cock. Mouth open, eyes closed, cheeks flushed, she was halfway to her next orgasm already.

I brushed my lips along her jaw, sucking at the place just below her ear that always made her go crazy. "And next week," I whispered against her skin, "we can go to The Beerhive and test out the waters. All friendly faces there, promise."

She pulled back, her eyes snapping open, and looked down at me. Even as she continued to rock against my hand, she pouted. "It's not fair to ask me that now."

I grinned, pushing my fingers deep. "I know."

She groaned, her eyes fluttering closed. "Fine, whatever. Now will you make me come?"

"Greedy girl, aren't you? You just came all over my cock, and now you wanna come all over my fingers?" But still, I gave her what she wanted, using one firm hand on her hip to guide her movements as she rocked over me, the other pumping my fingers inside her.

She worked herself faster over me, pressing down against the head of my cock as she stilled over me, her whole body going taut, mouth open, head thrown back. "Connor…"

Jesus, hearing my girl say my name while she shuddered on top of me, her pussy squeezing my fingers as she came? Didn't know if there was a better feeling in the world.

"That's it, beautiful. Love making you come."

I kissed her temple, using soft touches to bring her

down until she was once again boneless on my chest, her contented sigh filling the otherwise quiet space.

Recalling her doubt over going to the bar, I tightened my arms around her, wanting to offer her reassurance. "You know that even if there weren't friendly faces at the bar, I have your back, right?"

"I know." She tilted her head to look up at me, smiling. "And I love you for it."

I'd been wrong. Hearing her tell me she loved me while lying naked in my arms was the best feeling in the world. I leaned forward and nipped her lips, unable to contain my smile. "If we don't get upstairs right now to get you food, I'm going to fuck you again."

"I'm not sure I see the problem here," she said, just as her stomach rumbled with an ungodly sound.

"Your monster of a stomach is the problem."

She laughed, swatting at my chest as she pushed up and off me, gathering our clothes so we could get dressed. The only thing that placated me as I watched her cover up her gorgeous body was knowing she'd be naked again as she fell asleep next to me tonight... and every night for the foreseeable future.

Once she'd gathered up a few things, including the envelope with her graduation present in it, we headed out. As I shut the door behind us, it only reminded me of exactly what I'd come upon earlier. I tugged at her hand as she walked up the steps in front of me, heading toward my—*our*—apartment. "Lo... for my sanity, I really need to know why you were in your apartment with your door open."

She didn't stop, didn't even glance back at me. "I was getting my mail."

"But the *door*, beautiful. Jesus, you're driving me crazy. You can't just leave the door open! Anyone can walk in. Please don't tell me you do this every day."

"It's the first time I've come down here alone since I basically moved in to your place, so, no. Not every day." Her laughter rang in the hallway. "You are such a grumpy, overprotective bear sometimes."

I blew out a relieved breath. "Yeah, well, I have this gorgeous girl I'd like to keep around for a very long time. I get to be an overprotective bear as long as it keeps her safe."

When she got to the top of the stairs, she turned and stopped me with a hand to my chest, pausing me two steps below her. "I love you for being so caring, even if it can be ridiculous."

Slipping an arm around her, I hauled her up against me and continued up the stairs. "You know how crazy it makes me to hear you say you love me?" I kissed her jaw, nibbled along the length of her neck. Bringing my lips to her ear, I brushed them along the shell. "Think I can make you come again in the time it takes for our food to get here?"

She laughed as she wrapped her legs around my hips. "I'm up for the challenge if you are."

With a grin, I carried her into the apartment, shutting and locking the door behind us. Prepared to show her just how up for the challenge I was.

chapter ten

LOLA

I'D NEVER THOUGHT being in a relationship could be so freeing. Every night, I fell asleep in Connor's bed. In his arms. And every morning, we had breakfast together before we separated to start our days. His shifts at the police station varied, but I kept busy with school and scouring the internet for potential jobs. I'd need money eventually, but I wanted to find the right position considering how long I'd been working toward my degree. Rumor's gift would keep me afloat until I found it. Hopefully.

High on the happiness being with someone who truly cared for me offered, I danced around our bathroom as I got ready for our date night. Once I had my favorite stretchy pencil skirt on, I grabbed one of Connor's sweatshirts I'd permanently borrowed from him and tossed it over my tank top. I loved wearing his clothes, especially when we went out. There was something comforting in knowing anyone could tell the shirts weren't mine. That they were too big, too masculine. That I had someone who cared enough about me to share everything he had with me. Plus, his were softer than mine, and they looked amazing over my skirts.

As I finished putting on my makeup, a knock sounded at the door. Connor didn't knock on his own door, and he wasn't in the living room when I stepped out to see what was going on. I tiptoed across the floor, suddenly nervous. Was the person at the door an old client of mine? Had someone tracked me down? What if Dave, the last John I'd gone to see, the one I had run out on, turned me in? Connor would be furious, especially since he wasn't with me. The man was cautious about me almost to a fault. A burly, overbearing, caring sweetheart who only wanted me safe and taken care of. And he obviously wasn't in the apartment with me.

Shit.

"Who is it?" I yelled through the locked door, grabbing my phone just in case.

"Open up, beautiful."

I yanked open the door, smiling up at Connor. "You scared me."

He grabbed me, wrapping his arms around my body and pulling me in tight. "The car's warming up, so I don't have my keys. Sorry."

"You're forgiven." I rose up to give him a kiss, one he deepened immediately. He moved his hands to my ass and pulled me off the floor, pressing me against him. Slipping his fingers under my skirt to tease the bare flesh of my thighs. Overpowering me as usual. And I loved it.

"Maybe we should stay in," he mumbled as he moved to my neck, kissing and nibbling the length of it. Making me shiver as his cold skin brushed against my warmth.

I was tempted—so very tempted—to say yes and avoid leaving the apartment, but he'd been so excited about us going out. He was giving me an out, a chance to keep hiding from the reality outside our walls. I loved him for it, but I couldn't give in. I had to be brave…for him. "Maybe we should go out instead, so I can tease you all night before you bring me home to that big bed of yours."

"Mmm…not bad, but my idea gets you naked sooner."

Charmer, for sure. Though he had a point. Still. "My idea gives us the opportunity to see how much we can get away with without anyone noticing."

He jerked back, those sexy blue eyes of his definitely interested. "No one gets to see that look on your face when you come. No one but me."

There he was, my overprotective bear of a man. "No one will. I'm sure there are a few convenient closets at the bar."

He blinked, staring, then his smile grew. "Such a dirty girl. I love it. Let's go."

My stomach knotted, the thought of leaving the safety of the four-plex something I'd been dreading.

But Connor was excited to see his friends, so I would go. And I would smile. And hopefully, I would stay as invisible as possible behind him.

We headed to the bar down the street, Connor driving the car he'd been warming up at the curb. God forbid I be cold on his watch. The bar was a local dive called The Beerhive, usually only frequented by other people who lived in the neighborhood behind the factory. There wasn't even a sign over the door or in the parking lot—nothing lit. Instead, there was a dark plaque taller than me on the wall with the name and the shape of a beehive in gold-toned metal. If you drove by, it would look like any other squat, brick building. But this one served burgers and alcohol.

I'd never actually been inside, though Connor was a regular. He used to invite me to go with him sometimes before we'd crossed that friend-to-lover threshold, but I'd never wanted to. Being in public always carried a risk for me. What if I was recognized? What if someone had seen my picture and knew what I did for a living? What if I got caught?

Nope. I wasn't a bar girl. But with Connor, I knew he'd make sure we had a good time.

The place wasn't crowded when we walked inside, the high-top tables mostly empty. But there was a definite feeling of camaraderie there. Everyone hollered a hello to Connor, all eyes darting to me as he held my hand and smiled. I'd never felt so exposed.

Connor must have sensed my unease, or he simply knew I'd be uncomfortable. He yanked me right into his side, keeping his arm tight around my shoulders.

Keeping me tucked in my own private nook as he escorted me across the room. As we reached the bar, he nodded at the bartender—a tall, skinny woman with bleached hair and an eyebrow ring who was wearing a *Muggles Gotta Muggle* tank top. I liked her immediately.

"Hey, Star. I'll have my usual, and she'll have a hard cider. You got the green apple ones?" He glanced down at me, his brow furrowed. "You're still drinking the green ones, right?"

I nodded, biting back a grin. The man knew me too well.

Connor handed the bartender his card to start a tab when she brought back the bottles. I took a sip of mine, thankful for the cold crispness of the alcohol. Needing it.

"They know you're with me," Connor said, almost whispering into my ear. "I know every single person in this bar right now. You have any problems, you can go to any one of them, all right?"

I nodded, my face burning. But the people of the bar, the handful of men and women I'd seen over the years in the neighborhood, all smiled when our eyes met. All seemed welcoming. Accepting me immediately as Connor's girl. A fact I took a lot of comfort in.

"Want to play Around the Clock?" Connor asked once he'd drunk about half his beer.

"I don't know what that is."

"C'mon, I'll show you." Connor grabbed my hand and led me to the back corner of the bar where three dart boards were set up. "Have you ever played?"

"No, but when I lived on the farm back home, I was pretty good with a throwing knife."

Connor's eyebrows shot up at that, his disbelief plain, and the telltale gleam of arousal in his eyes caught my attention.

I leaned back, cocking my head. Unable not to give him my are-you-kidding-me look. "You can*not* be that easy."

"I'm always easy where you're concerned."

Rolling my eyes, I grabbed one of the darts from the case he'd set on a table. There was more heft to them than I'd have thought, but still, nothing compared to what I was used to. "What am I trying to do?"

"How about we start with you hitting the board, badass." He leaned against a barstool, grabbing his beer and bringing it to his lips. His thick, soft, pink lips. The ones that could do such naughty things to my—

Nope. Back to the game. Hit the board. Right. I refused to get distracted by the way his shirt sleeves pulled tight across his biceps or how his pink tongue flicked out a second before the glass bottle touched his lip. I refused to fall prey to such obvious tactics.

I really should have worn jeans. I had a feeling my skirt was going to give the man ideas. Hell, if I was super honest with myself, I was looking forward to when those ideas came to life.

Focusing on the board, I gripped the dart between my fingers and thumb. Connor suddenly came up behind me, his big body pressing against mine, his hands—as usual—finding their way to my hips. Tugging the fabric of my skirt up my thighs a little.

"Twist." He tugged on my hips, forcing me to move my body to face the board at more of an angle. "Light and easy. It needs a little power to stick, but if you give it too much, the dart will bounce back. You have to get the right pressure."

Dammit, the way he said that last word. The sexual sort of whisper he used. He was trying hard to break my concentration. It wouldn't work, couldn't. I needed to throw the dart—to get one to stick.

Connor had his thumbs under my tank top, rubbing along the waistband of my skirt. Pressure? He wanted to talk about pressure? I'd show him pressure. I leaned back into him, making sure to press my ass against his cock. Teasing him with a little extra rub.

"This good?"

He groaned and dropped a kiss on my shoulder, sneaking a quick bite as well. "So good."

Taking a deep breath, trying hard to focus on the board and not the way Connor was slowly moving his hand up toward my breast under the giant sweatshirt I wore, I aimed, pulled back, and released. The dart flew through the air, landing with a thump on a black section with the number twenty along the edge.

"How was that?" I spun around, grinning, elated the dart had stuck.

His smile was huge, the expression on his face one I couldn't turn away from. One of love and pride and heat. "Good, beautiful." He pulled me close, giving me a quick kiss. "Just what I'd expect from a knife-throwing rock star."

"Ecuador is not for the faint of heart, my friend. Someday, I'll take you to see the farm my family owns. Teach you to be the one throwing the knives."

"I wouldn't miss it. Now how about you try to throw another one?" His hand was back under my shirt, his thumb brushing against my nipple and making me want to moan. "Try to hit the nineteen this time."

And so started the longest, dirtiest game of darts that little bar had probably ever seen. Connor's hands roamed under my bulky shirt, and I made sure to pay attention to his cock with any part of my body that was close enough. He helped me improve my throw by plastering his body to my back and rocking his hips with mine, and I argued his counting method was off while stepping between his legs as he sat on a barstool. I couldn't keep my hands off him, and luckily, he seemed to feel the same way.

Two hard ciders and three beers into the night, our private bubble evaporated. In a good way.

"Connor." A man walked into the dart area, one who looked an awful lot like Connor. Supersized. "Good to see you."

"Hey, man." The two met for one of those back-slapping man-hugs, breaking apart when two women walked into the room. Two I recognized.

"Where have you been, stranger?" A girl with wild light-brown curls smiled up at Connor, her shirt riding up as she reached to hug him. I knew her from school, from a couple of my business-track classes. A younger woman stood to her side, her long, dark hair accenting her pale skin and puffy, pink lips. Another one who looked familiar.

"I've seen you around campus, right?" I asked the dark-haired girl.

She smiled softly, almost appearing shy. "I think so, yeah."

Connor stepped up at that moment, pulling me into his side. "I'm sorry, beautiful. I'm an ass. Everyone this is my girlfriend, Lola. Lo, this is my little brother, Riley, my baby sister, Claire, and a friend of the family, Evie."

"Hi," I said, doing my best to give them all a wide smile. Connor was introducing me to his *family*. Somehow that felt so much more important than even us moving in together. So much more real. They all greeted me and seemed nice, too. That was definitely something to smile about.

As the two guys signaled for more drinks, Connor turned his attention to the dark-haired girl—Evie, he'd said—even though his hand kept playing at the place where the waist of my skirt met my stomach.

"What, no Nate tonight? I thought he got off at nine."

Evie shook her head as she settled herself on a barstool. "He got stuck doing some paperwork. He'll be here soon."

"I can't believe he let you come up here without him."

She shrugged. "I told him I'd be with Riley and Claire. He was fine after that."

Connor raised his chin once in acceptance, then

leaned down to kiss my cheek and whisper in my ear. "There's no way he was okay with anything. You think I'm overprotective? Nate takes it to a whole other level with Eve. Not that I can blame him." He slid his hand up higher, pulling me closer. "When you find the woman of your dreams, there's no way you'd let anything happen to her."

"Yo, Connor," Riley yelled from across the room. "Let's play some darts."

Connor never turned away from me, though. "In a minute."

I stared up at him, feeling warm from the drinks but also from him. From having his love shine on me the way it did. From the sensation of being his, being protected, being cared for in ways I'd never imagined. This man...

"I love you, Connor," I whispered, running a finger along his scratchy cheek. "I really do."

"Love you, too, beautiful." He kissed my nose and gave me another squeeze before heading off to play darts with his brother.

The room grew louder and more boisterous, the men taking over the dart games and talking smack to one another as they threw. So much like how my own family interacted. I missed them like crazy, missed family dinners and weekends like this where we were all together. Seeing Connor and his siblings in that same light warmed my heart and reminded me of what a family really was. I sat against the wall, just watching them—taking everything in—a cider in my hand and my eyes on the Nash kids.

Happy. Comfortable. And a little tipsy, if I was being honest.

"What did you do for the holidays?" Evie asked as the guys came over to grab their beers.

"Family as usual," Connor said with a shrug, thumbing toward where Riley and Claire sat arguing over whose bottle had more beer left. "Listening to those two arguing, and food for days."

Evie turned her attention to me, still smiling. "What about you, Lola?"

"Oh, I don't celebrate much." When they all stared at me blankly, I rushed to fill the suddenly awkward silence. "I don't really have anyone here. My family moved back to Ecuador as soon as I graduated high school. Holidays aren't the same without family to celebrate with, so I skip them…mostly."

Evie's face pinched into an uncomfortable expression, and she simply nodded before moving on to another topic. Connor stared at me with a pained expression on his face, and I knew that caretaker side of him was doing a number on his attitude. Something I could help with.

"Stop," I whispered, leaning in close. "I never told you how I spent my holidays because it didn't matter all that much to me. It's fine."

His frown only deepened. "Next year, we're getting the biggest fucking Christmas tree on the island."

My laugh was loud, my hands clinging as I reached for him. "Whatever you say, boss."

He yanked me closer, cornering me. Pulling me

right into his body once again. "I'd like to take you home and show you how much of a boss I can be."

I stole a kiss from him, sucking his bottom lip between my teeth for a moment. "Later. Enjoy your time with your family."

Connor looked as if he was about to argue, but Riley called him back to the game.

"Go. Play." I squeezed his hand and slid off the barstool. My legs wobbled a little, and the room spun for that first second of being upright. Yep, a little too much to drink, but in that good way. Tipsy was fun.

"Where you going?" he asked, getting far more handsy with me than was probably appropriate considering people could see us. Tipsy Connor was fun, too.

"Bathroom." I brushed against him as I passed, making sure to run my fingers over the front of his jeans as I did. "Maybe I'll see you in a few."

I didn't wait for Connor's response to my teasing. Instead, I headed straight back toward the sign on the wall that said restrooms. The hall to the bathroom was long and dark, but it wasn't hard to find the ladies' room. Single toilet, sink, mirror, and a dim overhead light—about what I expected. I hurried through what I needed to do, wanting to get back to Connor. Excited to spend time with his friends and family like a normal couple. He'd been right—this bar was all his people. I felt comfortable here, safe, didn't feel like I was under a microscope. Hopefully, we'd spend more time here.

I washed and dried my hands once I was finished,

fluffed my hair, and was just unlocking the door when someone shoved their way through it instead.

"What the—Connor?"

He shushed me with a finger to his lips, locking the door behind him. And then his hands were on me, tugging my clothing out of the way, pushing me back toward the wall. "You've been teasing me all fucking night. I need to have you."

There was no question in my mind about what would come next. "Then have me."

chapter eleven

CONNOR

ALL NIGHT HAD been an exercise in restraint, and Lola had loved torturing me. Brushing her hip or her hand over my cock, pushing her ass right up against it. Combine that with seeing her in my sweatshirt and one of those stretchy skirts she loved—the kind that just barely peeked out under the hem of my hoodie— it was a wonder I hadn't fucked her up against the wall next to the dart board. I'd passed the point of needing her a good hour ago, though I hadn't wanted to push. But when she'd given me the green light, all bets were off.

Lola didn't protest when I backed her against the wall, sliding my hands under my too-big sweatshirt and the tank she wore to cup her tits, kneading them as she shimmied out of her panties.

"I've spent all night thinking about fucking you."

She hummed, pressing against me as she rucked up her skirt to her waist, baring her pussy to me. Even pushed up on the balls of her feet, she was too short to get anywhere near my mouth, though it was clear she was hungry for a kiss. With two handfuls of her ass, I hauled her up against me.

She smiled, kissed me, but pulled back before I could deepen it. Bit her lip as she looked up at me with hooded eyes. "I've spent all night thinking about sucking you off."

I groaned, gripping her ass tighter and grinding her against my cock currently attempting to fight its way out of my jeans. "Jesus, beautiful. Don't say that."

"Why not? It's true."

This time she let me slip my tongue between those full lips, deepening the kiss. It was hot as fucking hell as she worked herself over on my cock. Like she was desperate to get it inside her. She moaned as she ground down on my cock, rolling her hips against me in the way she did when she was horny as hell.

Jesus, I needed inside her. And soon.

"You know I love your mouth on me, but I'm not letting you get on your knees in this bathroom."

Her bottom lip poked out in a pout. "Fine, but I'm totally taking your cock in my mouth when we get home."

I pinned her to the wall and worked my jeans open, pulling out my cock and quickly sheathing it, thanking every deity I could think of that my girl had made sure my wallet was always stocked with condoms. "You're already wet for me, aren't you, sweet girl? Soaked the front of my jeans, didn't you? I'm gonna walk back out there with your come all over me and love every second of it."

With that, I gripped her ass and pulled her down on me as I slowly worked my way inside her tight pussy—short, shallow thrusts, inching my way deeper each time, always stretching her—groaning into her skin with my face buried in her neck.

Lola gasped once I was seated fully, sliding her fingers into my hair and holding me to her. "Connor…"

Knowing we'd already been in here too long, I pumped into her the way I knew would make her come, and come quickly. She'd spent all night teasing me, working me into a frenzied state. It wouldn't take anything to get me to go off.

"Lo…my girl. My beautiful girl. Love being inside you." Reaching between us, I settled my thumb on her clit, flicking it back and forth in time with my thrusts. Lola tossed her head as she clamped down on me, her moans no doubt loud enough to be heard through the door as she came, taking me right over the edge with her.

"Shit," I groaned, her pussy squeezing my cock as I pulsed inside her. "That's so good. So fucking good."

She kissed my neck, then gripped my face, bringing it up until I could press my lips against hers. "How does it keep getting better?"

I smiled at the awed tone of her voice. Thanking my luck that I'd somehow found her and she'd somehow agreed to be mine. "No fucking idea, but I'm not questioning it."

We left the bathroom once we'd cleaned up, Lola walking ahead of me. With her fingers linked in mine, she turned around, glancing back at me with a smile as she tugged me along behind her. Truth was, she could tug me anywhere, and I'd follow. That girl had me wrapped around her damn finger, and I wouldn't have it any other way. Loved every goddamn second of it.

I brought her hand to my mouth, pressing my lips to her fingers. "Love you, beautiful."

Too focused on the way her eyes lit up as she stared at me, how her dimple dented her cheek, proving exactly how happy she was—how happy she was with *me*—I didn't see the guy heading toward us until he was right there. In her space.

"Oh, excuse me," she said as she bumped into him, spinning around to look at him. Her hand went tight in mine, her entire body frozen.

"Well, look who we have here. Thought you didn't do this on the island," he said, herding her toward the wall. "What's this treatment cost?"

I tugged Lola toward me, not thinking about anything but getting her away from him. Needing her behind me. Needing her safe.

"You got a problem, asshole?" I stepped up to the guy, going nose-to-nose with him. It was then, when I was close enough to catalog his traits, that I recognized him.

"Connor, let's just go." Lola tugged on the back of my shirt, trying to get me to walk away.

But I couldn't. I *couldn't*. The night in the alley came back in the blink of an eye. His hands on her wrist, squeezing. Leaving bruises. His much larger body holding her against the brick wall of the building. Her eyes wide and fearful.

With clarity, I remembered every detail, the seconds of that night ticking by in slow motion. It wasn't just the fear on her face in that moment, it was her entire demeanor. She'd been unhappy, and until that very second, I hadn't realized exactly how far she'd come. I'd be damned if this asshole did anything to take her back to that. Would fuck him up simply for daring to dim her shine.

"She let you fuck her in the bathroom?" he asked, whiskey soaking his breath. "How much extra she charge for that? She told me that was off the table."

I saw red, even as she pleaded with me to stop, tugged me back, trying to get me to walk away. I couldn't. I didn't stop to consider anything past shutting him up. Didn't think beyond getting him away from her. Needing to keep her safe.

Hands braced against his chest, I shoved him hard, forcing him out of the hallway. Forcing him away from Lola. "The fuck did you just say?"

He stumbled backward, barely righting himself from falling on his ass. "Who the hell do you think you are? Don't you know who I am?"

"I don't give a fuck who you are. You don't get to speak about her." I shoved him again, hanging on to the last thread of control that prevented me from swinging. From knocking this fucker out. "You don't get to even fucking look at her, asshole."

"Hey, she's the one for sale. Her price tag says I can look all I want."

My entire career revolved around the fact that I was cool when faced with a volatile situation. I didn't ever lose my temper, had never been out of control. I'd spent years on the force, been in countless situations requiring me to keep my head. And I had, for every one of them.

But none of them had ever threatened my girl's safety. Any ounce of control I'd managed to keep up until then snapped as soon as the words left his mouth. Despite Lola at my back, begging me to let it go. *Please, Connor, please.* Despite the fact that I was a cop about to start a bar brawl, knowing damn well it could end in my suspension—or worse. None of it mattered.

Lola was mine to protect, not just from actions taken against her but from words. From *shame.* I didn't care what she'd done in her past—hell, I didn't care if she'd role-played with a John an hour before coming into the bar with me. I wasn't going to allow anyone to disrespect her. To make her feel like goods instead of a person.

Because of that, I didn't think about anything other than shutting that fucker up as I pulled my arm back and snapped it forward, connecting my fist with his smug face.

chapter twelve

LOLA

THE THUD OF Connor's fist hitting the man's jaw almost made me sick. I screamed, my hands coming up to cover my face, but it was too late. It was really, really too late.

"Break it up, now." A cop—wearing the same uniform pants and department hoodie I'd seen a million times—jumped between the two men, pushing Connor back. He hadn't been in the bar before we'd headed to the bathroom, so he must have just arrived. He must have… oh my God, had someone called him because of Connor and me in the ladies' room? The guy Connor punched— the potential client I'd met that one, stupid time—knew exactly who I was and what I did. What I'd done.

He knew me as Lolita, and I had no doubts he would tell everyone. And Connor was going to lose his damn mind.

I was watching my life end in real time. All I could think of, all I could focus on, was Connor facing down the police officer in front of him. Connor was pissed, his body language radiating the fact that he was in his over-the-top protective mode. He was going to say or do something to defend me, and there really was nothing to defend. The guy had called me a whore, and I was one. Or had been.

I'd been trying to start over again, but apparently, that plan had just failed. Completely.

"Someone want to tell me what's going on here?" the cop said, eyeing everyone in the crowd hard.

My stomach twisted, guilt a heavy noose around my neck as his eyes skated over me. Something there, something in the way his eyebrow rose and his jaw ticked, told me he knew who I was. What I was. I had no idea how, but I could tell. And that made me feel even worse.

"Officer, I'm Preston Welding, and I want to press charges against these two," the man Connor punched said as he pushed his way to the front of the crowd.

He pointed toward Connor, something that enraged me. I stepped forward, ready to defend the kindest man I'd ever known, but Connor dragged me behind him again. Ever the protector.

"What kind of charges are you thinking about filing?" the cop asked.

The Welding guy lifted his chin, gesturing toward Connor. Toward me. "He assaulted me because I witnessed a crime."

"What sort of crime?" The cop arched an eyebrow,

watching Welding with interest. This was bad. This was so very bad.

And somehow, as Welding's eyes met mine, I knew it was about to get worse.

"That woman is a prostitute turning tricks on the island—"

Oh sweet Jesus…

"I told you to shut your fucking mouth," Connor said, leaning forward as if to charge. I grabbed his arm, pulling him back.

"Don't," I hissed, trying and failing to hold him in place. To keep him still so he didn't make things worse. Not that things could get much worse. Thankfully, Riley jumped into the fray, grabbing Connor around the chest and manhandling him away from Welding.

"See?" Welding said. "He's a damn animal. When I tried to tell someone they had a whore working the room, he attacked me. Almost knocked me to the ground in a rage."

"I've already seen how you treat women, you lying bastard. You left bruises on her the last time you had her penned up against her will. If you think I was letting you do that again, you're a goddamn idiot. And I'll show you fucking rage, just keep calling her a whore."

The cop held up his hands, silencing both men before turning to look at Connor. "What's your story?"

Connor clenched his jaw. "It's bullshit—"

"Not you, kid." The cop tipped his chin at me. "You. What's your story?"

My mouth went dry, and my heart nearly exploded in my chest. My story? I was a college student, a woman on her own with no family to back her up, and an ex-sex worker. I had a feeling that last part would be the worst to have to admit, but I would if it meant Connor wouldn't get into trouble. Wouldn't lose his job.

"I…uh—"

"She's with me." Connor reached back, his hand wrapping around mine. "She's mine."

Something passed over the cop's face, and his eyes flicked behind me. I had no idea who or what he was looking at, but there was a break there. The smallest moment of something soft, and then he glowered again.

Before he could say another word, though, Riley grabbed me by the shoulder in a supportive sort of way. "Lola wasn't working anything. She's Connor's girl. And it's like Connor said, Officer. That guy"—he pointed at my almost-client—"had her trapped in the back. Connor was only defending her."

I stared at him, my mouth almost falling open. There was no way he saw that, and everyone in that bar probably knew it. Everyone but the cop, who regarded Riley with something close to apprehension. But then the bartender chimed in.

"I saw the same thing. That young lady was in trouble, not coming on to him. Connor helped her."

Claire appeared as well, standing firm right beside her brother. "Same here. Connor was trying to get the guy off her. She wasn't doing anything wrong."

Connor wrapped his hand around her arm, supporting her. Pulling her gently behind him as he had with me. He was protective of her in a way I hadn't noticed before, though I understood it. He'd told me how she'd been attacked, how he'd found her. I wanted to hug her, to thank her for standing up when she probably just wanted to hide, but it wasn't the time. For the moment, I could only focus on the danger of the situation. The consequences of the cop believing Preston over Connor. Claire and I could commiserate another day.

Some older lady who'd been sitting in the back corner with no way to have seen what happened spoke up next. "The guy had it coming. He had that poor girl trapped. Connor had every right to defend her."

And another. And another. One by one, everyone in the bar joined in the chorus of defense of Connor. In the defense of me. No one corroborated the charges Welding tried to claim, no one went against the story of Connor defending me from an attack. Until the only silent person left, Evie—who had probably been closest to the hallway to see what had kicked everything off—came to stand beside me.

She even grabbed my hand. "That man attacked Lola, and Connor defended her. You'd do the same for your girl, wouldn't you?"

The corner of the cop's lips twitched, whether to fall into a frown or rise into a smile I had no idea. "You want to file charges, Lola?"

I leaned into Connor, shaking my head. "I just want him to leave us alone."

Welding looked over the crowd nervously, obviously feeling a bit outnumbered. As he should have. "I'm telling you, she's nothing but a—"

But the cop had had enough. "A woman who could easily press charges for assault and battery if you don't shut the fuck up." He looked up at Connor. "What about you? You good?"

Connor took a deep breath, his hand squeezing mine. His shoulders tight as he nodded once. "If she's good, I'm good. But he needs to get the fuck off our island."

The cop grabbed Welding by the arm. "I think that's the best idea of the night. C'mon, Preston. I'll call in a squad car to escort you to the bridge."

"But I bought a ferry ticket."

"That ferry doesn't come for two hours, and your time on Temperance Falls is up." The cop shoved him out the door, looking back once and almost catching my eye.

"What just happened here?" I asked, tugging on Connor's arm.

"Not yet, beautiful," he said, pressing a kiss to my temple as he watched the door. "Wait until he comes back in."

I stood and waited as I was told, Connor holding me against his side with his arm securely around my shoulders and Evie holding my hand. No one made a sound, no one dared to move as we all stared at the door. The entire bar seemed to be holding its collective breath. By the time the cop walked back in a few minutes later, I was a shaky, terrified mess.

"You," the cop said, striding to Connor with long steps. "'She's mine'? You stealing my lines?"

Evie laughed and let go of my hand before running at the cop and wrapping her arms around his neck. "You made it."

"Just in time, apparently." The cop leaned down and kissed her, a possessive hand resting on her ass. "Sorry I'm late."

"The Nashes and Lola kept me company."

The cop's eyes swung my way again, and I tucked myself into Connor's side purely out of habit. "Lola, I presume?"

Connor's hand on my back supported me, giving me enough security to offer a soft, "Hi."

"You okay?"

Connor squeezed me closer, dropping his hand to my hip. "She's fine, Nate. I was there."

The cop smiled. "Good job, kid." He tugged his department hoodie over his head, revealing a white undershirt pulled tight across his muscled chest, and stretched his neck from side to side. "I need a fucking beer."

It was as if his simple statement restarted the world. The bartender hurried behind the counter, rubbing a hand across my shoulder as she passed me. More people took the time to walk by, to say quiet words of support, to offer a hand or a touch. No one mentioned the truth Welding had said, no one seemed to care that I might have been a sex worker at one time. All that mattered to them was that I was Connor's, and that made me one of them. And as

Nate and Evie joined our group in the dart room, as everyone went back to telling stories, drinking beers, and throwing darts, I snuggled into Connor's side and rested my forehead against his chest.

"You remember what I said when we walked in?" he asked. "I meant it. You're mine, so that means you're part of this crazy family we've got here. And we protect what's ours." He pressed a kiss to the top of my head.

I didn't even notice the tears falling until he wiped the first one away. "Hey…hey. Why are you crying? Are these good tears?"

I couldn't have held back my smile if I'd tried, and I didn't want to try. "These are the best tears."

Wrapped in his arms, warm and safe exactly where I wanted to be, there was only one more thing to do.

"Can we go home?" I asked, leaning back.

"Anything you want." He tucked me into his side again, his arm heavy on my shoulders, and headed for the door, throwing a hand in the air to wave goodbye when the group started yelling to him.

"Should I say thank you or something?" The wind had picked up, the night colder than when we'd arrived. I pulled my thick coat around me even as Connor bent his body to try to block me from the gale.

"You can say thanks next time we go there. They'll be okay with the wait. Besides, I want to get you home."

"Trying to get into my pants, Connor?"

"I was already in your pants." His smile was soft,

relaxed. Maybe relieved. He tucked me into the car and pulled the seat belt across me. "When we get home, I just want to hold you."

He closed my door and hurried around to his side of the car, slipping into his seat mere seconds later. "Okay, *first,* I want to hold you. Afterward, there might be fucking. I haven't licked your pussy yet today."

"Oh, the horror. However do I put up with you?" I laughed, reaching for his hand, grinning when he brought it to his mouth to kiss the back. And as he started the engine and fiddled with the vents, I said a quiet prayer of thanks for all the bounties given to me. For the first time in my life, I could honestly say I felt like the luckiest girl in the world.

epilogue

CONNOR

I PULLED OPEN the front door of city hall, nodding distractedly at the couple of people who called my name. I was too focused on getting to my girl to pay much attention to anything else. Needing to see her. That wasn't new—I could barely wait to see her at the end of her day or after a long shift. But today was different.

Today, she was meeting my parents.

Lola had put it off for weeks, always giving me an excuse as to why it just wasn't a good time. She was too busy with classes. Too focused on finding a job. And I knew that'd been a major concern of hers— being able to tell my parents what she did for a living and not having to lie.

As of two weeks ago, she'd officially become the administrative assistant for Mayor Briscoe, and she loved it. Loved interacting with people, loved putting her skills to use. She was happy, but more than that, she was fulfilled.

Walking briskly, I turned the corner into the doorway to the mayor's outer office, which housed Lola's desk, colliding with someone coming from inside.

"Sorry, 'scuse me." I pulled back, noticing the familiar face of my brother. Brows drawn together, I said, "Riley? What're you doing in the mayor's office?"

He glanced behind him toward the closed door that led to the mayor's private office, then focused back on me and gave a shrug. "Wrong turn. I was paying a ticket. What good is it having a cop for a brother if he can't get me out of tickets, anyway?"

My brows drew down. Besides the fact that everyone on the force knew my family and wouldn't give them a ticket without letting me know, something in Riley's body language was off. He was edgy…agitated. Totally and completely unlike him. I clapped a hand on his shoulder. "Everything okay? Lo and I'll still see you tonight for dinner, right?"

He glanced again toward the mayor's closed door. "Yeah, yeah, for sure. Everything's fine. Just have to make a quick stop, and I'll be over. See you in a bit." He walked out, leaving me in the room by myself. I'd have to ask him later at dinner what was going on, but right then, I was too focused on seeing Lola to dwell on it.

Her desk sat empty, but I didn't have time to worry about where she was before she came around the corner, looking hot as hell. Those damn tight, stretchy skirts she loved to wear did a number on me—especially since the night in the bar three months ago. I couldn't see her in one without remembering what it'd been like to have her pressed against the wall, coming all over me in two minutes flat.

I walked straight to her, hands gripping her ass, and tugged her against me. "You look hot as fuck in this. Have I told you that?"

She laughed against my lips. "I believe you mentioned something about it this morning before you dragged me back to bed."

"I'm sure Mayor Briscoe would've understood you being late." I bent my head, nipping at her neck, focused solely on my girl, the rest of the world falling away.

At least until a throat cleared in the small space, breaking the trance.

Lola pushed at my chest, shoving me away and smoothing her clothes. "Mayor Briscoe, I'm sorry. Connor was just—"

She waved a dismissive hand. "Greeting his girlfriend the way every girl can only hope to be greeted." She pulled her coat off the coatrack and slipped it on. "I'll see you tomorrow, Lola. Officer Nash. Have a good night."

After the mayor walked out of the office, Lola buried her face in my chest. "I can't believe she walked in on that."

With a gentle touch, I ran my hand up and down her back. "Look on the bright side, beautiful."

"What's that?"

"With our track record, it could've been a lot worse. Besides, I'm sure she doesn't blame me. She has eyes. She sees how gorgeous you are."

She pinched my side, causing me to jerk away with a laugh. "Not helping, Connor."

"Sorry. How about if I help you get your coat on instead?" I grabbed it from the hook and held it out for her. "We've got twenty minutes to get to my parents', and I wanted to stop and pick up a bottle of wine on the way."

"Damn. I was hoping you'd forgotten about it," she said as she slipped her arms into the sleeves of her jacket. "Or they canceled. Or your car broke down so we weren't able to go."

I snorted, wrapping an arm around her shoulders as I pressed a kiss to her temple. "Too afraid you'll hate them, huh?"

She looked up at me as I led her outside to my waiting car, rolling her eyes. "You know that's not the problem."

"What I know is you're out of your mind if you don't think they're going to be crazy about you."

Once she was settled in her seat, I shut the door on any argument she was going to come back at me with. That was short-lived, because as soon as I slid into the car, she twisted in her seat toward me.

"What if they…figure it out? What if they already know what I did for a living?"

"Lo…my parents are in their sixties. They're not exactly on the pulse of the nightlife on the island." I reached for her hand, rubbing circles with my thumb. "You've already met Riley and Claire, and they both love you."

"But you sprung them on me with no notice, and besides, this isn't your siblings. This is your *parents*. I already have to deal with a mom who sees you as one of her babies and will hate me on sight for taking you away from her. Having to do that as a former call girl isn't exactly making my life easier. What if they ask questions? What if they can sense the"—she waved her hands, obviously searching for a particular word—"the sex worker? Connor, what if they can tell?" She shook her head, hiding her face, picking at the edge of her skirt as if that loose thread held the secret to life. "They'll hate me."

"Beautiful…" I reached over and brushed her hair back from her face. Traced the curve of her cheek like I'd once only thought about doing. Leaned in and pressed my lips to hers, just because I could. "They're going to love you. Do you know how I know?"

"How?"

I wrapped my hand around the nape of her neck, pulling her toward me. Letting my lips settle against hers with a single soft kiss. "Because *I* love you."

It was as simple as that. Family protected family. Family loved family. If Lola made me happy—and she did, more so than ever before—then my parents would love her.

She sighed against my lips and rolled her eyes. "Fine. I'll take your word for it. But if your mom kicks me out for sullying the good reputation of her first-responder oldest son, that's on you."

"I'd be more worried about them kicking us out for fucking in the bathroom, honestly."

"Oh my God, Connor, we are *not* having sex in their house!"

I laughed at her outrage. Bringing her hand to my lips, I kissed her fingers. "Fine, I'll give you a pass for the introductions. But all bets are off for future visits."

She didn't say anything, just shook her head at me. As much as she wanted me to buy her irritation, it wasn't working. She could pretend she was annoyed all she wanted, but that dimple didn't lie. I reached up, stroking it with my thumb, and she bit her bottom lip to stifle her smile.

"Ready?"

She pulled away, staring at me for a moment as her eyes darted between mine. Then she took a deep breath, gave a short nod, and squeezed my hand. "Ready."

Her acquiescence was weighted, and I understood the importance of it. She trusted me, completely, knowing I wouldn't lead her into a den of lions. And even if we somehow ended up there, I'd protect her however I needed to. Standing by her side as long as she'd let me.

Forever, if I had it my way.

She's the one thing he won't give up on

The calls started a year ago. I needed an easy release, and he was there, for a price. One call turned into two, and before I knew it, I was falling for the voice on the other end of the line. When he shows up and introduces himself as the newest firefighter on the island, I'm terrified...at first. As the mayor, the last thing I need is a scandal. But Riley won't take no for an answer, and I'm finding it hard to refuse him.

He's a distraction he can't afford

Kate, the mayor of Temperance Falls, has a naughty little secret. Except I'm not so little and a hell of a lot more than just naughty. A year of weekly phone calls with our identities disguised has left me craving more. Being together could ruin everything she's worked for, but there's no turning back. Now that we've actually met, now that I've had a taste, nothing will stand in my way of making her mine.

about the author

London Hale is the combined pen name of writing besties Ellis Leigh and Brighton Walsh. Between them, they've published more than thirty books in the contemporary romance, paranormal romance, and romantic suspense genres. Ellis is a *USA Today* bestselling author who loves coffee, thinks green Skittles are the best, and prefers to stay in every weekend. Brighton is multi-published with Berkley, St. Martin's Press, and Carina Press. She hates coffee, thinks green Skittles are the work of the devil, and has never heard of a party she didn't want to attend. Don't ask how they became such good friends or work so well together—they still haven't figured it out themselves.

www.londonhale.com